STARSHIP INVINCIBLE

STARSHIP INVINCIBLE

Science Fiction Stories of the 30s
by Frank K. Kelly

A Noel Young Book
Capra Press
Santa Barbara, 1979

Copyright © 1979 by Frank K. Kelly.
All rights reserved.
Printed in the United States of America.

"Crater 17, Near Tycho" first appeared in *Astounding Stories*, June 1934.
"Star Ship Invincible" first appeared in *Astounding Stories*, January 1935.
"The Radium World" first appeared in *Wonder Stories*, February 1932.

Cover design by Mary Schlesinger.

Library of Congress Cataloging in Publication Data

Kelly, Frank K   1914-
  Star Ship Invincible.

  "A Noel Young book."
  CONTENTS: Crater 17, near Tycho.—Star Ship Invincible.—The radium world.—The crisis with Mars.
  1. Science fiction, American. I. Title.
PZ3.K29615St [PS3521.E4235]   813'.5'4   79-9076
ISBN 0-88496-140-0
ISBN 0-88496-139-7 pbk.

A Noel Young Book
CAPRA PRESS
P.O. Box 2068
Santa Barbara, California 93120

STARSHIP INVINCIBLE

CONTENTS

Foreword / 7

Crater 17, Near Tycho / 15

Star Ship Invincible / 51

The Radium World / 101

FOREWORD

Leaping to the Stars — and Worlds Beyond

ONE world has never been enough for me. The stars have beckoned to me since I first walked alone at night and saw silver spangles glittering in a black sky. It seemed to me that all those stars—and the planets around them—were there to be explored by voyagers from earth.

The stars to me meant glory—the splendor and bliss of heaven on high. I yearned for those burning lights, for those great fires in the dark fields of space. I was an intensely religious boy, and I believed that I was bound for glory.

It seemed to me that man would leap to the stars before visitors from other planets arrived on earth. I did not fear encounters with them, but I realized that tremendous dangers lurked between the stars. There might be black holes into which a traveller seeking the limits of heaven might suddenly fall.

My first teachers were Catholic nuns who taught me that the immensely powerful God who had made the stars had also made me. This God loved to make stars and people and millions of other things—and He loved everything He made. He had created me to love him and to know him and to serve him, and to be happy with him forever. Yet there were perils which had to be faced.

These nuns taught me that there were angels and demons around at all times. Invisible warfare was going on around me and around us all. There were dark powers and principalities seeking to devour me, and resplendent angels defending me. I was very important to God—and the Devil.

My favorite teacher was a beautiful nun who was not frightened by the questions I asked. She encouraged me to write stories, to let my mind run freely, to leap toward the stars if I felt like leaping. She told me that God had given me some of his creative power, some of His courage, some of His strength. To be a man, I had to be brave and strong.

She assured me that I would reach the castles of heaven if I persevered. But I might have to go through a long night of the soul. I might be tested, I might be disappointed, I might have to suffer great pain, I might have to go down into a valley of tears. In order to rise to the heights, I might have to fall into the depths.

The stories I wrote in my teens reflected these ideas—and my own absorption in the possibilities of science. When Lindbergh flew over the Atlantic, I knew that some day a man could fly to the moon—and to the worlds beyond. I read H.G. Wells and Jules Verne, and I was sure that man would soon escape from the boundaries of the earth.

In 1927, when Lindbergh flew alone from New York to Paris, I was thirteen years old. I wrote several stories about lonely heroes who soared to Mars and Jupiter. My first critic was my father's father, known to me as Grandpa Mike. He read my tales, chewed on his white mustache, fixed me with a stern stare, and snapped his verdict: "Too damned many superfluous words." I took his advice and reduced the number of my adjectives.

One winter day in December, 1930, when I was sixteen, I wrote a story about two scientists who had developed a device to bend light-waves and entered another universe where they were attacked by Monsters. I called it "The Light Bender" and sent it to Hugo Gernsback, who had begun to publish *Wonder Stories*, which he described as "the magazine of prophetic fiction. I was then working in a box factory, twelve hours a day. My father had lost his job in the Depression and I had been forced to go to work as soon as I finished high school. I was lucky to have a job, but I hated it.

Four months went by. I thought my story had been lost in the mail. The world for me was dark and dreary. Then I got a letter from Gernsback. He had accepted my story and sent me a check. The world for me was bathed in light again.

"The Light Bender" appeared in the June, 1931 issue of *Wonder Stories* with this statement by the editor: "Man with his tremendous development of science may be considered as a child fumbling about in the dark of a great cavern. He stretches out his hands and finds things that he puts to his own use and they serve him well. But the nature of the things that he finds and uses is still a mystery to him, and as he plumbs deeper and deeper into nature's laws to find new devices for himself, he may be intruding into a world that he does not understand.

"So science may easily prove a boomerang to man, and destroy him in the process of civilizing him. Our brilliant young author has taken this theme and woven it into a finely conceived . . . and gripping story."

In my story the scientists tested their light-bending device in the Peace Tower, a New York skyscraper three thousand feet in height. I wrote: "It had been born in an inspired time—the years immediately following the holocaust of the Third World War of 1990 . . ." Why did I, in a story written in 1930—long before the rise of Hitler to power in Germany, long before the outbreak of World War II—assume that there would be three World Wars? Perhaps it was because my father, who had been severely wounded as an infantry officer in World War I, had gloomily told me that the Germans would try again to dominate the earth.

In any case, I was delighted to find myself described as "a brilliant young author"—and Gernsback offered me a contract to write six stories a year for his magazines. Soon after I received this offer, my father found a good job and he gave me permission to leave the box factory. I began to write stories on a typewriter my parents gave me. I taught myself to type, and pounded the keys at a furious rate.

I wrote a dozen science fiction tales in the years between 1931 and 1935. While the United States was going through an economic collapse, while millions of men were standing in bread-lines, while Hindenburg and Hitler were fastening a dictatorship on Germany, while President Roosevelt was proclaiming that the only thing Americans had to fear was fear itself, I was traveling to other worlds. I was plunging from planet to planet and leaping from star to star.

When I entered the University of Kansas City in 1935, I encountered a professor who told me that science fiction was a minor form of art, not worthy of my talents. Unfortunately, I believed him. I began to write other kinds of stories. Many of these were published, too, but I stopped producing tales of the future.

In gathering the stories for this collection, I went over all of the wild adventures which poured from my mind in the dark and troubled years of the 1930's. And I discovered that these stories were full of excitement, full of the passionate fantasies of a romantic young man who believed in the courage and heroism of human beings, who was sure that men would try to conquer all the planets and all the stars, that men would encounter beauty and horror, defeat and triumph, the hunger for love and the need for sacrifice as they voyaged through many universes.

In a sense, the drama in "Star Ship Invincible" is closely related to the tormented plight of the scientists in "The Light Bender." The people in "Star Ship" cross the boundaries between universes—and fall into the grip of darkness. Those in command of the ship decide who will have a chance for life—although what kind of life it may be, no one knows—and who will die at a certain moment. There is a struggle on the ship between those who show the power of love and those who make cold scientific decisions.

"Crater 17, Near Tycho" was described by the editors of *Astounding Stories* as "a tale of the space-ways, and an outlawed ship fighting against the deadly problem of weight." But it also has the atmosphere of revolutionary fervor, a feeling of a desperate conflict between people on the Bottom Levels and their rulers. And it is a story about a man who sacrifices his life for his friends—and tries to deny that he is being a hero.

I will not try to analyze the other story in this collection. In different ways, all of my stories grapple with what I consider to be the greatest mystery in all the universe—the mystery of consciousness. Man is a collection of dancing atoms, shaped into molecules clinging together. Man is made of the same stuff as stars and rocks, elephants and oceans. But man is aware of what a strange being he is.

How does it happen that self-awareness arises from the dance of atoms—awareness of oneself, of the stars, or worlds to be explored? How can a collection of molecules fall in "love" or experience "hate", or sit down and write a book, or compose a symphony, or build a Star Ship designed to be "invincible"?

How can the small assembly of gray matter in the head of a tiny creature dwarfed by giant suns and planets develop ideas of galaxies and infinite swarms of stars? The answer is really beyond the grasp of scientists and philosophers, as Einstein and others have admitted, and I think it will always be beyond the grasp of all of us. But we cannot keep from searching: we must always reach beyond ourselves.

The excitement of the endless search is in these stories, which reflect my conviction that man is intended to fulfill a great role in the evolution of life. There is a basic truth in the statement that man is made in the image and likeness of God.

After my religious youth, I became convinced for a while that science had eliminated the idea of God. God was dead and could not be revived. While I believed that, I wandered through a long night of the soul. I did not think it would ever end, but it did.

Through experiences which shocked and overwhelmed me, I came back to the ideas of my youth. I felt the presence of God as a creative Being, a Father-Mother capable of everlasting love—capable of being incarnated as a Son of Man, capable of pouring out His Spirit of Wisdom upon human beings of all nations and tribes, all creeds and colors. The heights and depths of many worlds emerged from this Creator, who flows through all things like a stream of music with infinite variations.

I became aware, too, that the heights and depths of many worlds are also in Man, who knows more than he understands, who sees his brothers and sisters as companions and rivals but flesh of his flesh and bone of his bones, who realizes that he is somehow separate and unique but still connected to the torrent of creative energy that shaped him and everything around him.

The thrust into space came at the right moment in humanity's history. At a time when man was overwhelmingly threatened by his release of atomic power, he discovered that he could escape from the earth. The stars he looked upon with awe might some day be within his reach.

A sad reader wrote to me once, after shuddering at the grim ending of one of my stories, and asked: "If a happy ending isn't possible in our solar system, how do you know it isn't possible under the light of another star?"

I believe that every ending, happy or unhappy, leads to a new beginning.

Through the far reaches of time and space, human beings will go through perpetual transformations. Our calling is to be sojourners and wayfarers, moving on and on.

These stories tell of some of the journeys I made in my mind and heart. There will be many more, for me, for you, for all of us traveling together.

—Frank K. Kelly

STARSHIP INVINCIBLE

Crater 17, Near Tycho

A tale of the space-ways, and an outlawed ship fighting against the deadly problem of weight.

I.

City of New York, 2021 A. D. Riot in Gotham Square.

UP past the swinging sweep of the city's great roof a rocket roared, hung poised in midflight, and expanded in a murderous mushroom of spitting green fire. Then followed the thin whine of an alarm siren, rising to a grating scream, dying away again in soundless crescendo as the range of its vicious vibration passed beyond the ken of human hearing. Then against the murky back drop of the night sky, blue fan lights began to prick, circling low, just skimming the rounded shoulder of the mighty roof.

Blue glare and white beam criss-crossed; the white beam rebounded searingly across the torn blackness and vanished, closely followed by an explosive echo, as of thudding thunder. The blue fingers of the giants' hands that seemed to claw the heavens thickened in answer, pushed upward more ascending columns of deadly azure brilliance in whirling clusters of light. The motors of distant patrol planes thrummed in sudden swift surge, like the beating of ten thousand drums, like the hammering roar of sea surf rolling against rock cliffs.

Loud-speakers blared, catching up the heavy overtones of an old man's spoken voice, tossing the sound out in great waves of concentric violence that spread in widened rings of noise over the city. The voice almost reached through the miles of space that stretched between the confusion and the banked slip-cradles of the interplanetary freight docks, perched high on the edge of the huge roof.

Almost, but not quite. It faded to a dim mutter here, like a behemoth growling hoarsely to rebellious midgets, with the last words swallowed in a backwash of innumerable tiny sounds, that grew swiftly to the roaring of a rising mob—

The small man sitting beside Rafe Brand jerked around nervously on a pivoted seat, and shot a disturbed glance out through the narrow slit of transparent glassite before him. From here, in the check tower of the great freight dock, the broken surface of the roof swept away into dimness. Flood lights hammered down in steady glare, etching the gleaming tracks of monorail trucks against a white background of thick glassite. Freight ships, dark and deserted, hugged the snug embrace of slip-cradles all along the dock.

Only one vessel, and that the closest to the ungainly tripod of the check tower, was agleam with light. The scarred sides of the black hull still glowed with red heat, still crackling to the friction-stress of atmospheric passage. The name glittered in luminous green letters: *"Isis,* Stellar Ship 946 RV, Cargo. Mars-Earth Cleared."

The check man shrugged and turned back to the clicking board in front of him. His swift hands played over the punch panel, keyed to the rising drone of his thin voice:

"176 tons, Earth Weight, beryllium. Mars checked, 943 kinolotts. Gravity loss, 1.43. Checked. Next way line—"

Brand leaned forward, bright eyes hiding the surge of feeling deep within him, head tensed to the sound and stir in the dim distance. He spoke in a husky voice: "What's breaking over there? Got the look of a first-class war."

"Maybe it is a war."

"I don't sniff the idea."

The other swung in his pivoted seat again. His eyes looked Brand over in swift appraisal; he saw a tall, solid space man, deeply colored by glare of sun and heat of stars, body corded with responsive muscles, dark fierce face topped by graying thatch of black hair. Stenciled across the tunic front of a shabby uniform were the words: "Freight Commander, Interstellar Corporation. License registered. Tape Spool 3876. Earth recorded."

After a minute the check man said: "You been away some place for a while, haven't you?"

Brand made a little motion with one thick hand. "A while, yes. You could say that. A long time. I've been cargoing stuff for Interstellar the last eight years. Since I got my license."

"What channel you been workin'?"

"Mars-Jupiter."

"Long jump."

"Yes."

"Just switch channels this trip?"

"Yes."

"Mind tellin' me your name?"

"The name's Brand—Rafe Brand."

The flat face of the check man relaxed. He nodded. "I got you. Mine's Garnet."

They touched hands.

"You asked me what was goin' on over there."

"I'd kind of like to know," Brand said.

"It's nothin' you could call new," the check man said. "Riot in Gotham Square."

Brand hesitated an instant, purposely not quite hiding the puzzled uncertainty he wanted to show in his eyes. The other leaned close, glanced once again around the narrow outlines of the check room, in a swift leaping jerk that took in everything.

"You look right to me, so I'll tell you something."

"Thanks," Brand said, allowing himself the edge of a smile.

"There's been a riot in Gotham Square every week for months. You oughta get the idea. It's the custom to give the Bottom Levels a chance to tell what they think about things, in a mass meeting called every seven days. Not that it means anything, of course. They talk, they do a lot of silly gassing—and the Controls shove the records of the meetin' away under a mountain of red tape. Nothing ever comes of it, see? The Controls just go ahead and do what they want."

Brand's face was very smooth and quiet, perfectly impassive. No muscle quivered to show that the man was telling him things he already knew. His head moved slowly.

"I believe I get you. A kind of safety valve. No meaning to the thing, the meeting, I mean—except to let off steam that might burst if they sat on it too hard. Smart scheme."

"Just that," the check man said, and grinned; but the grin twisted his thin features in a bitter outline.

He watched Brand narrowly, almost with suspicion. He was sorry he had talked. Better not go too far, with this silent man from space. Didn't know who he was. Might be a Control. Couldn't tell him you had a son who'd got too much in the open during a riot in Gotham Square—and died, with the sour smell of an ion beam burning through his lungs. Better keep a tight mouth, keep it buttoned.

"Just that, smart scheme," the check man said again. "Only it hasn't worked out just as they figured it. The Levels have raised merry hell. They've forced the Controls to give them representation of one man in the upper council. To-night they say they've discovered their representative, Gagin, has sold them out."

"You mean—" Brand began, and paused. His lips laced tight, and he nodded. His mouth moved soundlessly, but the other caught the thin echo of muttered words: "The dirty piece of static space!"

"I call him the same thing," the cargo checker said, grinning.

Brand said: "Call him what?"

"Didn't you say something?"

"No."

"All right," the checker said, still grinning.

Brand stared as if he hadn't heard, his face blank and smooth again. The small man turned around, and began to work at the controls of the infra-penetrator. Brand watched, one half of his brain tuned to the meaning of the other's words with their undercurrent of quivering bitterness, the remaining half taut and strained, concentrated on the dial readings of the infra's mechanism.

He jerked his body closer to the shut circuit of the control switch; if this check man was on his job, drove the searching infra-beam in through the thick stellite hull of the *Isis* to the aft hold, brought out in clear outline what lay there, that would then automatically be recorded in cargo files with photographic clearness.

It was Brand's unswerving resolve that the check beam would not sweep through the *Isis* again. Already it had gone once, half power, preliminary check—and come dangerously near to the secret of the cargo ship, deflected off the aft hold only by the smooth flow of the interference stream that had been set up there. But the dials had jumped and jerked, registering an obstruction, and only the sound and confusion in the distance had kept the checker's suspicion from speedily rousing. Hard thing, this was that he had to do. Hard to turn on this unsuspecting friendly man, drive the butt of his electronic pistol into the base of the thin neck, snap out the other's little life—but he could take no chances. There was more lying in the balance now than one little man's life.

The checker was speaking again nervously, eyes on the distant flurry of lights, his narrow body tensed to the flare and burst of police rockets, his thin ears tuned to the wail of screaming sirens.

Brand stiffened a little, leaning forward. "Think the Bottoms have any chance of winning?" he asked. The resolution was half formed in his mind to give the other a chance at longer life. If he spoke now against the Controls—

The small man hesitated, looking at Brand queerly. "Not a chance in hell. No more chance than a space man with a smashed oxygen tank, two thousand miles off side his ship. The Control police will wipe them out."

"I think so myself," Brand agreed gravely and hid the tightening purpose in his eyes. The check man would have to die.

So the little man thought the Control police would wipe the Bottom Levels out with ion beams and paralytic gas, and fire shells smashing downward! Well, his mind might change if the penetrator drove through to the stacked cargo in the aft hold. Row on row of small stellite containers lay there. And inside them—odd-shaped things, harmless enough in look, deadly in sting: the coiled deadliness of the Martian sound oscillators. Hundreds of them, charged and ready.

Even the Controls wouldn't have a weapon that could stand against the Martian whirling death. Sound fields that dropped down in singing streams and ripped the atoms of matter apart, swung them wide in racking confusion. Oscillators tuned to the vibration level of human bodies, that could maim or kill at will.

Brand's eyes jumped to the smooth dial of the chronometer on the wall above the penetrator control board. One fifty-eight, Eastern terrestrial standard time. And Gar had said they would meet here at two.

Gar would have men, trusted and sworn to the cause of the Bottoms, to muster up the sparse ranks of his own space handlers, now waiting quietly in the central cabin of the *Isis*. Swift transfer of small heavy containers to purring mono-trucks, an interchange of instructions, and Gar would be gone with his cargo of death. And the *Isis* would be swinging up again through silent space, roaring out past the city's roof to meet the curved arch of the black sky. There were men in the crater stations of the Moon, sickened of the tyranny of the Controls, eager for battle. The *Isis* would come back crowded.

Brand sent his glance past the shoulder of the cargo checker, through the glassite slit in the wall of the narrow room. He saw the gleaming ribbon of stellite that marked the path of a mono-car. One track was humming, swaying to the furious passage of a heavy body. He saw the coming car, glittering under the flood lights—a small, blunt-shaped object, shifting rapidly through the distance.

The check man was intent on his work and did not see. He was reaching out a thin hand for the control switch of the penetrator, his high voice beginning to drone: "All right, Brand. Preliminary check complete—"

His voice died, cut off in a sudden choking silence. Brand's hand rose once, fell hard, bronzed fingers wrapped about the thick hilt of his electronic pistol.

The little man stiffened, head lolling, the glaze of quick death creeping in behind his blank eyes. He dropped forward, limply crashing against the dull metal of his control panel.

Brand shoved the gun back inside his uniform in a quick flick of the wrist, then turned, stood just at the edge of the low doorway, shivering a little. Not easy to kill a man like that—take him from behind, without warning, without a chance to fight back. And yet any other way might have meant failure.

Failure for the millions under his feet, the Bottom Levels of a top-heavy civilization, the base of the human pyramid. The millions deeply buried under tons of stellite and glassite, living and dying out of sight of the Sun and Moon, oblivious to the slow march of white stars in the purple pageantry of the night sky. Not to breathe clean air, nor see the Sun, the glory of it. Not to smell the warm odor of the Earth in spring, nor stiffen to the whining whiplash of winter winds. Not to be a part of the world's ancient heritage. All that was denied men, unless they were born in the circles of the upper councils, unless they were of the Controls— Well, all of that was going to be changed.

The distant mono-car was coming fast, the rail shivering to the smash and flash of the speeding projectile. Suddenly Brand stiffened, stared with dark, incredulous eyes, his fists clenched at his sides. A sharp foreboding of disaster struck him—the car was too small to hold the men Gar had promised to bring. Then something had gone wrong.

II.

It was close enough now for Brand to see the insignia stamped on one round gleaming side of the car: "One Man. For Freight Only." Something wrong! This must be Gar coming to tell him—

It was. He knew that at first glimpse of the slight figure of the man below, that tumbled in wild haste out through the snapped-open door of the mono-car, and came panting up the narrow ladder of the check tower.

Terror was riding the man under him—beating a tattoo in the quick *spat-spat* of the running feet, the harsh, ragged murmur of the other's gasped breath. The dark head turned and looked up, caught the outline of Brand's body in the doorway.

"Rafe! You're here!"

"I'm here," Brand said slowly. "But your men—the men you promised you'd bring—"

"Gone, all gone! The fight I've had, making it out this far—"

Then Gar was there beside him, swaying a little, his grim face green and white under the cold impersonal glare of the roof flood lights. A red stream dribbled in a zigzag flow along the drawn skin of his jaw, cascaded down across the split lips. One arm of the dark man was hanging queerly at his side, swinging limp and useless.

"Steady!" Brand said quietly.

He caught the thin shoulders, held the other braced for an instant, let him catch lost breath. Then Gar straightened and nodded, and jerked away. The tight lips moved, formed into what was the shadow of a smile.

He said: "All right now. I can take it."

"Sure!" Brand said. "Sure, you can!"

He waited.

After a minute Gar said: "We've got to get away from this place. Got to go now. Before they finish us both. The *Isis* can take off again, any time?"

"Yes," Brand said.

Gar passed a trembling hand across a white face. "The riot started to-night in Gotham Square when—"

A picture leaped in Brand's mind at those few words. Gotham Square. Not a square at all, but a huge cavern in the depths of the Bottom Levels. Seats, ring on ring, tiered mountain-high. Packed with the thousands that were lucky enough to fight, steal, or beg a way in. Surrounded outside, in dimly lighted corridor, by the millions of the city canyons. A raised stage, with microphones and amplifiers for the speakers. A jutting dais, the place of honor, for Gagin, honorable representative of the lower people in the Control councils.

Gar muttered: "It was awful! Massacre!"

And Brand said, quietly: "Better tell me what happened."

But some deep instinct in him told him that he already knew. Gar was talking again, in a high-pitched voice, words and sentences tumbling out through a nervous mouth in rapid flight, incoherent, breathless, yet somehow shaping a vision of chaotic pandemonium that had been.

The news had seeped through, down to the lowest levels of the city, to the half men who lived in almost complete blackness, that Gagin had sold his vote to the Controls. And this night Gagin was there to speak to his people.

Gagin was there. Pale-lipped and jerky-eyed, and with fear quivering in every line of his body—but there, under the fierce eyes of the crowd, which sat in thunderous silence, harshly staring. Others were on the platform, a few score of them, including Gar, a handful brave enough to mock the wrath of the Controls by setting themselves up as an advisory group to the Lower Levels.

Gagin made a speech. Not, Gar said, a speech really at all, but a muttered gibber, hideously distorted by the man's terror. The crowd had remained quietly through it all, until the finish; at the end there was a little silence—a terrible stillness in which no one moved or spoke.

Then the crowd went berserk. And Gar had gone along with them. Quick, light, swift-fingered, his hand had gone to the needle pistol at his belt, come up, flashed in a sputtering arc of flame, tearing into Gagin's shuddering body. Behind Gagin a rocket flared, rising up past the mob in a flaring burst of scarlet glow: in the crowd there had been someone sent by the Controls. Sirens whined, wailing through the packed corridors of the canyons. Helicopters dropped from above, plummeting down through a widened opening in the city's roof, fire shells and ion arcs slamming in hot flight before them.

"I got away," Gar said softly, and shuddered under Brand's hard grip. "I got away. Came here. How—I've forgotten. I stole a mono-car, broke through that mob, got up on the roof—"

His voice died, came again in a great burst: "I killed Gagin. They'll get me, some way."

Brand sought Gar's one good hand, crushed it in a long, slow pressure that spoke more than all the words he knew and gave evidence of all that came crowding to his tongue.

He spoke slowly: "You're sure no one saw you come across the roof—followed you?"

"I told you. I can't remember."

"I know," Brand said. "But you think—what?"

"I think they did," the other muttered, the words flat and dead.

His eyes were on a spot beyond Brand's shoulders; his glance swept out to the dark sky. Lights stirred and whirled in that sky, shifted with the purring hum of helicopter motors; white beams stabbed down across the roof.

"They're coming now."

Brand stood up straight and faced the scarred hull of the *Isis*. "Then we'll fight with what we've got, old son—and go down battling."

The other's bloody hands went up to his face. "No. Rafe, don't you understand? That's why—I killed Gagin."

"What do you mean?" Brand demanded.

"I believed in him, told him what we were going to do. I told him about the oscillators, about you. And he carried it all to the Controls, let you walk into this. This is the trap they set for you."

Brand struck his fists together. "They don't know what they're walking into. We'll do what we can—with the oscillators. We'll take some of them with us when we go out."

"Even that," Gar said numbly, "we can't do. The alloy. The X stellanium isotope in the coils isn't—"

"You mean—it's not there?" Brand said. He stood stunned.

Gar muttered: "I mean that. It's not there."

Brand fought the rising surge of despair that swept up in his throat, choking him. He stirred, whirling on the other. "For all that, Gar, we've still a way left clear. The *Isis* is space-ready. If they try a blockade, we'll break through."

Hope wakened in the slight man's dark eyes. He hesitated an instant, as if considering. Then:

"You're right! We'll take the *Isis* and hit out for the Moon. The Controls haven't taken over the crater stations yet. I didn't have time to spill that to Gagin. Rafe, if we could do it—"

"No time to talk now," Brand said swiftly. He was standing on the first rung of the check-tower ladder. "Down with you. Varney's standing by. He expects to pick us up—but not for the reason we've got now. We were waiting here to unload the oscillators."

"I know."

Gar nodded, and followed him down the ladder, swung across the smooth floor of the great roof, moved up the rising ramp that led to the cargo ship's cradle. Brand flashed the signal. The huge gimbaled door of the airlock began to swing on balanced pivots, turn inward, give a glimpse of the lighted interior of the freight vessel.

The lock stood open. Dan Varney, Brand's tall second in

command, halted in the doorway, staring. Brand swung an arm behind Gar's shoulders, helped the other up across the lock, into the control room of the *Isis*.

He jerked round on Varney. "We've got to get action, Dan. Bad break. Gagin sold out to the Controls. Gar, here, came to warn us. Police fleet overhead. Get the lock closed and take us upstairs."

"Blockaded above?" Varney asked slowly.

"Don't think so, but might be."

"If we are?"

"Break through. Use forward ram."

"We're going out of the atmosphere?" Varney asked quietly, his hard brown face unchanged and impassive. If he felt any amazement at this sudden turn of things, he didn't show it.

Brand hesitated an instant, not looking at Gar. "How are we on space supplies?"

Varney shrugged, drawled: "Fair. Might make it."

Brand flung his voice out in a sudden burst: "Then hit for the Moon."

"Where on the Moon?"

"We'll base at crater 17, at the edge of Tycho."

Varney gave a flicking gesture that was as much of a salute as Brand ever received from him, and turned, swung across the close, metal-walled room to the handling set-up of the freight ship. Giant Donlin sun engines began to turn over, build up pressure for the huge backlash of energy that would stream out behind and send the *Isis* hell-driving up through open space. Light glowed on the small face screens of the ship's individual visa plates and died again as Varney finished giving orders to each member of the ship's crew.

Brand walked straight to the big television panel at the side of the airlock, dropped into the comfortable bucket seat before it, shifted directive dials. The scene above and outside the freighter showed in sharp, clear outline—the silent check tower, with the crumpled body of the check man dimly visible, dangling limply over the top rung of the descending ladder; the pale ribbon of the mono-track, stretching away to nowhere; the flood lights hurling down showers of cold glare.

And above in the distance, contrasts in the black mirror of the sky, heliships were drumming on in massed flight, white beams flashing nervous fingers out before them. They were close now, closer than they had been when Gar and Brand had fled down the check-tower ladder. Even through the thick sound-insulated hull of the ship the roar of packed motors came rumbling. The crackling crash of ion beams searing through shuddering air smashed against Brand's eardrums.

He swung on Varney. "Got any pressure?"

"Pressure building," Varney snapped laconically.

Brand looked at Gar, still standing dazedly by the closed panel of the lock. "Strap yourself in there," Brand ordered, pointing to the curved outline of a chair equipped with acceleration compensators.

The other obeyed quietly.

Brand gave the "General Attention" buzz on the ship's communicating web, spoke crisply to unseen men standing by in compressor rooms and firing chambers:

"Give me pressure. And remember we're not taking off easy. That's all. Emergency stations."

"Pressure, sir!" Varney roared from across the room.

Brand tersely nodded. "Shoot it through, all channels!"

"Everything we've got?"

"Everything we've got!"

Varney's heavy fingers danced over the gleaming studs of the control board. A split second of no response—then roaring speed, coming into action. Plumes of repulsion streams stood out in long peacock fantails behind the exhaust nozzles of the thundering ship. Brand watched sky and roof and distant stars go whirling by in glittering confusion. Then it was over. The *Isis* zoomed through the Earth's atmosphere, crashing through screaming air, scarred sides red-hot with friction stress.

"Below!" Brand yelled in triumph. "Look below!"

Gar followed his eyes. Below and behind massed helicopters fluttered in baffled rage, stabbing out hot fingers in blue beams of swift force that almost touched and scorched the speeding freighter—almost, but not quite. The *Isis* was gone before the beams crossed in liquid fire.

Gar lay limp in his seat, crumpled under the crushing shock of sudden acceleration piled on top of his already weakened body. Brand got up, went to him across a firm floor held steady by gravity grids under stellite plates, made a swift examination.

Gar was knocked out. Brand picked him up gently, carried him past the visa screen and through a narrow door, into the officers' sleeping cabins. Then Gar was taken into Brand's own room, after the freight captain had finished some rough, quick surgery. A broken arm and a sore jaw—nothing too deeply hurt for repair.

Varney was waiting for Brand when he came out and closed the door.

The other faced him with grave thin eyes. "What happened, back there?"

The captain told him, in brief, sharp strokes that drove it home. When he was finished Varney said in a soft voice:

"This doesn't mean anything—after what he did on Earth—but it's something we've got to figure on, Brand. We weren't counting on an extra man for this trip."

"No," Brand said slowly; "you're right, there. We weren't. And we were expecting to pick up some stuff to carry us back over from Gar's end of the line."

He was silent an instant, meeting Varney's eloquent eyes. "We'll go easy, understand? We'll stretch what we've got, both ways from the middle. We can make it go a long way."

"Sure!" the other said, very low. "Well, it might last—but if it doesn't?"

"If it doesn't," Brand answered, looking straight at him, "one of us will have to—drop out."

III.

They both knew what that meant. Varney jerked a little, then straightened, his face falling into set lines. It took—nerve. Yes; you needed nerve to take your last look on the bright face of life and say good-by deliberately to all life meant. You stripped, made the slow walk to the emergency lock—and then were shot spinning out into the frozen blankness of interstellar vacuity. There were a few men brave enough to do that—if it meant a chance for a better life to millions; if it meant that there would be some left to—well, carry on, to fight again.

"Right," Varney said gently; "I see what you mean."

They fell silent after that. There wasn't much more to say. Hours swung past, measured out by the ceaseless click of the little chronometer in the wall; hours, counting by Earth time—nothing at all, here in space.

The Earth, that had been concave, now changed, melted first to an indistinct outline obscured by clouds, then assumed the round convex bulge of a great ball slightly flattened at the ends and bulging in the middle. Varney kept sending the pick-up beam of the televiser back through infinity to the bright Earth, fingering out to contact the first distant shimmer of movement in the void space behind them—movement that might indicate the coming of the Controls' ships in dogged pursuit of the freighter. Nothing stirred. All quiet. The freighter drove on through nothingness, engines thrumming, compressors sobbing and groaning under the hard load of top speed.

Figures changed and multiplied in Varney's cold brain. Calculations, integrations, all the abstruse formulae of space-time navigation. The *Isis* could do one thousand Earth miles per hour, with maximum freight load. One thousand! And the light ships of the Controls could make three with ease.

They had no chance—unless there was a long delay and the freighter took too big a lead. Even then, if they were carrying an overload of one man—

They took alternate watches. First Varney for eight hours, Earth-recorded; then Brand; then Gar, sore from his bruises, his battered head still topped by a white crown of bandage. Eight hours each they spent strapped into the control seat, eyes taut on the winking panels of the great directing board, fingers and hands busy at switches and studs. Eight hours free they had, to study the televisor screen, to talk, to drop down the engine-room ladder to the compression chambers and firing compartments, to think. That was the worst—thinking. But they had eight hours' sleep; and, sleeping, sometimes they forgot—

Brand touched Varney lightly on the shoulder in the middle of the third day, nodded, and took over. The tall man stood up lithely, muscles stretched, grave face relaxing in a long yawn.

Brand sat down, swung the revolving dials, tensed his eyes

for a first glimpse of the white Moon on the lookout plate just above the control board. Crater 17, near Tycho. That was refuge. If they got there, they were through untouched. The Controls might know they were on the Moon, might make an effort at finding them, might savagely search; but the Moon wasn't mapped and zoned and guarded as the Earth; there were wild places untapped by the visa beams of the Council patrols. Crater 17, near Tycho—

Varney spoke in a low voice from behind Brand, startling him. The tall man was staring at the complacent face of the chronometer. "More than two days, Brand. And no sign of their coming after us. I actually think—I actually believe we're going to make it."

Brand nodded slowly. "Yes. We've held even at about one thousand per, all the way from atmosphere. Thirty-six thousand miles—gone. And still we're not yet close to the Moon—if the patrols come out here, hunting us—"

Varney rubbed a hand slowly across his lips. "I know. But we've been lucky. Maybe the luck will stay with us. Air's holding out. Food's lasting. The men aren't grumbling any more than usual. We've even a little water to spare, now that I changed the set-up in those condenser coils."

"Yes," Brand said again.

Varney noticed how drawn the other's face looked in the faint light of the control room. They had cut down on the juice that fed the cold globes, even though that was so little, to save power for the recoil streams.

Brand took his eyes from the unchanging glimmer of the directing board; he shot a glance across at the closed door leading to the sleeping cabins. Gar was off watch and asleep.

"Varney, get this. And tell me what you think. But quietly. We don't want to let Gar know until we have to, if what I've noticed is true. And it is true. The air's not holding. It's going bad. You've sensed that?"

Varney exclaimed sharply. His face whitened; he shuddered a little. Then he caught a grip on himself. He could be as big as Brand. Yes.

He took a heavy breath, drew a long draft of the ship's air into his lungs, and it made him sick. It was acrid, sour, with a rank staleness that spoke of its being used over and over again—passing through many men's bodies, expelling itself in a burst of lung effort, emerging charged with carbonic gas. Building up its percentage of that stifling gas, until it could be used no longer. Slow death would follow then, death by smothering, by suffocation—unless the air was changed, cleansed, made fresh again by the oxygen compensators.

Varney came to a sudden full realization of what a delicately balanced mechanism this ship was. Like most space handlers, he had taken it all for granted; it worked, because it was made to work. Well, maybe in a few more years men would be laughing at the crudities and inefficiencies of these hard-shelled monsters of thick stellite; maybe! He knew they would be, some day in the future. But not now. It was still new, this going out into space in a precarious bubble of welded metal, pushed forward through a void by forces little understood even by those who used them. Men had many things yet to learn about the space between the worlds.

Ships had conquered it, driven out across nothingness even from planet to planet, carrying men in numbers, loaded with what man called useful machines and weapons and supplies, complex mechanisms that made life livable in the roofed craters of the Moon, even on Mars.

But there were ships always being lost. Ships that got out of touch with beam-communication stations and drifted from known channels into some unknown limbo of forgotten space—and never came back to tell what they found there. Ships that broke down in mid-voyage and hung helpless between the pale planets, circling like small new worlds, starved satellites, until the men within them went mad and destroyed themselves—or fell back in a long dive against the hard face of a mocking Earth.

There was a balance that must be held in every ship, no matter the cost. Varney remembered reading of the first primitive submarines that cruised Earth's waters. It had been like this, underseas. So much air; so much space to move around in; so much food; so much to drink. It was that way here, in the void—a balance of interdependent factors; a balance nicely calculated between the crew number and the air used and the food consumed and the water absorbed. That was on one side of the equation; and on the other, the storage supplies and the power built up to carry the ship from world to world.

Something clicked in his mind, like the separate pieces of a picture puzzle falling together into one whole. There were eight in the crew. Counting himself and Brand, the ship carried ten. It was built to carry ten. No more. But they had Gar now. One man always left over. One too many. That left the equation uneven. It destroyed the balance—

He faced Brand, eyes smoothed out, hiding what he felt. He said slowly: "I'll have a look at the compensators. If we can pull a little more oxygen out of them—"

Brand nodded, a little more briskly, displaying a faint hope. "Even if we've got to cut down on what goes into the recoils, we'll have to do that. We can't live out here with no air."

Varney jerked a brief salute and was gone down the ladder to the machine room. He picked his way carefully along the metal plate of the catwalk, cautious not to put his feet down outside the laced grids of the protective flooring. Gravity compensation had been blocked off outside those grids—saving power.

He stopped slowly, stood facing the compact mechanism of the oxygen compensators, a quick glance jerking up along a narrow row of dials to a curving cylinder of transparent glassite. A warm opalescent fluid gently stirred against the bottom of the gleaming cylinder.

Varney's lips tightened; he bent down, touched the controls of the indicators. Looked up again. Waited for the response. None came. The compensator was dead.

A long time he stood there staring, his lungs struggling in the thick atmosphere of the aft section of the ship, his eyes beginning to smart from the effects of the rancid air. His vision was not as good as it had been; objects a little distance away he saw as through a slowly descending curtain of fog.

He raised his hands and looked at them. They were cold. His blood circulated sluggishly. He felt an uncomfortable weariness in his legs and arms.

Something stirred in hesitant movement behind him. He turned indifferently; the action roused him a little. His mouth went angrily taut. It was one of the firing crew; a thin, small man with a huge head and slitted flickering eyes.

Varney said: "What's this? What're you doing this far forward?"

As he spoke he shifted his body slowly, to hide the indicators of the air restorer, but the quick glance of the little man was there before him.

The other said in a thick voice: "I come to find out about the air. We're finding it hard, back aft. You got to shift a little power from the compressors. If you don't—"

Varney's frown tightened as he recognized the man. "Jorgensen! You don't mean—mutiny?"

Jorgensen shrugged. The pointed little eyes met Varney's confused glance. "I ain't said that, sir. But we're all a-havin' trouble with the breathin', and we can't think none too good. We got to have better air, or we ain't gonna be able to hold pressure."

Varney relaxed and nodded. He moved aside, giving the other a clear view of the needle readings on the compensator dials. "Then take a look at this thing, and you'll see the reason we've all been having trouble."

The little man barely glanced at the squat mechanism. Dropping his eyes, Jorgensen said: "Beginnin' with what you spoke last, sir, I think that ain't the reason for our trouble."

"No?" Varney asked harshly. "Then what is?"

"We've got one man too many aboard here."

The chief officer looked at the other in a sudden burst of scorn. "You mean you're not willing to take a little bad medicine with the rest of us—you're looking around for a Jonah already?"

The smaller man said in a low voice: "Puttin' it to you plain, sir, one of us has got to drop out through the E lock of this ship. When that's done, we'll be right again, and we won't have no more trouble."

"I see," Varney said softly. "So it's that simple?"

"Yes, sir."

"Who would you like to be the hero?"

The little man looked up, his eyes hitting Varney in the face. "We're every one of us aft ready to take our chances with the rest of your forward group, sir. If the captain asked for volunteers, I'd offer to go myself."

"I really think you would," Varney muttered.

"Yes, sir."

Varney saw that he meant it. His face was steady and still, and the sharp little eyes glinted in it like points of unchanging stellite.

Varney straightened back his own shoulders. "I'll speak to the captain."

"Yes, sir."

"Now about the compensator. Think you can fix it?"

"No, sir."

Varney stared at the set face. "Sure of that?" he asked quietly.

"If you want it straight, sir—there's nothing to be done about the compensator."

"Hopeless," Varney muttered, as if to himself.

"Yes, sir. The bottom coils are burned out."

"I understand," Varney said softly. "Return aft. I'll send for you, all of you back there, when the captain is ready to make his decision."

"Right, sir," the other said.

He had vanished before Varney could speak again, his slim body jerking in between the clicking mechanisms that filled the long room. At the far end of the catwalk a door opened for an instant; the lurid light from a compressor chamber flared out in a circular spot of flickering glare, then was gone.

Varney swung, on legs a little bit unsteady, and returned along the narrow metal path, following its windings back to the base of the flat, straight ladder leading up into the control cabin. He climbed the ladder very slowly.

IV.

Brand was doing something at the control board, shoulders bent, face and head hidden and savagely absorbed, fingers pulsating over shifted studs. Varney walked up quietly behind him, touched his arm.

Brand jerked round like a cat, his eyes flaming. "What the hell!"

For an instant he didn't seem to know where he was. Then he said: "You didn't change the set-up on those compensators this quick?"

"No," Varney said.

Brand flared: "Then what are you doing back here?"

Varney waited a little and then answered: "There wasn't any use changing the set-up, chief."

"Why?" Brand demanded.

"It wouldn't do any good. The lower-coil system is gone, burned out, trying to carry a constant overload. Oxygen's not getting through now, at all. No good trying to do anything with a break like that."

There was a change then in the way Brand looked, so deep and indefinable that it was only partly reflected on the surface of his eyes. He just looked a little more tired, his eyes went back a little deeper in his head, and his lips closed tight—that was all, but when it all was added up it made a big change.

"I thought we were due for something nice about now," Varney said; he grinned. The grin was unpleasant to look at.

"I've got a cute surprise, too," Brand said. "A swell thing I'm going to spring on you. But I think I'll wait till I hear what else you've got to say. You've got something else, haven't you?"

Varney nodded. "Yes. Yes; I have."

He stopped as if something held his voice. Then words came to him again, flat and strained: "I met Jorgensen, looking over the compensator. The men know about the air. They're having a bad time of it aft. They're asking you to—"

"Of course," Brand said, holding his face still. "They're crying because we're carrying just one man too many. And they want me to ask somebody to walk out and leave the party, so there'll be more fun for those of us who are left. Am I right?"

"You're right," Varney answered.

Brand knew there wasn't much to talk about now. Now it was in the open, and they all had to stand up and face it. Face it—face what? To go out alone into space. To be stripped, fitted into the emergency lock, and shot projectilelike into indifferent infinity. That took a little bit of nerve.

Brand raised his head. "Now let me show you what I've got for you," he said. "In some ways, it's a better joke than what you brought me. Look there."

Varney stared at the scintillant screen. He saw what was

shown on that glimmering bright surface, but his mind didn't really take it in. He knew it was there, the screen didn't lie, it was just a clever mirror to show whatever came within range of its activating beam—yet he didn't believe the message of his own eyes.

But it was true, all right. On the screen lay the clustered glitter of a Control space fleet, driving out from the spurned Earth directly in the path of the fleeing *Isis*. Speed and power and grace and gray, gleaming bodies, swiftly overhauling the slow freighter. And the air in this ship fast going! No; not going, either; the joke was bigger than that—the air was being poisoned by the workings of their own lungs.

Varney laughed.

"Don't do that," Brand said, shuddering.

"Sorry!" Varney jerked. He glanced down at his hands. "You were right. This is a better joke than any I know. Let me go first. I'll do it gladly."

Brand sat a little while in silence, looking at Varney. Then he unstrapped himself quietly, locked home the automatic controls of the freighter and came over to where Varney stood. He held out one hand slowly. "I've believed in you, friend, and I haven't been wrong. But you're not going. Shake hands with me once, will you?"

Their fingers locked, broke, and parted.

Varney said: "I'm the one to do this dance, chief. Who's better fitted for the job?"

"I am," Brand said heavily.

Varney shook his head. "You? Not you! You'll be needed, to break the Controls, as some day they're going to be broken. When we finish what we started out to do this time. Gar? He's needed, on Earth. Sometime soon he'll be able to go back, and he'll lead his people. He's got the brain and the force and the power to lead them, and when the hour comes they must be led. Now for me, I'm ready to take on anything. I've got nothing behind me that I'd care to cling to; and nothing I can see just ahead that would be worth more than my chance to do this. You know—I've wondered, now and then, how it would really feel to step out there in the great open places—alone."

Brand said, savagely: "Very pretty, but all wrong."

"Why all wrong?"

"Dead wrong," Brand said. "You're our navigator. Forgotten that?"

"You can navigate," Varney said, and he laughed a little. "Forgotten that?"

"I can navigate," Brand said, "but not the way you can. With you, the ship has a double chance to pull through. To get to Tycho with Gar and the men and keep the fight going. That's all any of us can ask."

"Yes; you're right," a slow voice spoke close to Brand's ear.

Brand looked startled, glanced at Varney, but Varney had not spoken. The door of the sleeping cabin was standing open, and Gar had come into the control room. He stopped, his head upright between his straight shoulders, his eyes watching them with faint irony. "This thing seems to be up to me," he said quietly.

"No!" Brand cried, his voice coming out of him in a protesting explosion.

Varney muttered something.

"Look, all the pieces fall in," Gar said, as if he hadn't heard either of them. "We'd have got away, clean, if you hadn't picked me up back at New York, Rafe. If I'd just warned you, and then ducked back underground, the ship would have gone straight through to Tycho, and no trouble. Now—well, we're pretty close to being finished—unless something changes. If we tried to fight it out, with the air getting bad and one man extra aboard, we'd get wiped from space. No heroics in this at all. There shouldn't be, if we all think straight. I'd like to go right now. No use in standing around and waiting until it's too late to do any good."

Varney and Brand stook silently looking at each other. When it had been thrown down in front of them like that, they both knew that Gar was right, that was the truth. There was no finding any way around it.

But Varney jerked his hand out in a little gesture and talked: "You've both left out something. The crew's in this. They're all Bottom Level men. It's their cause as much as ours. We've no right to deny them a chance to say what they think about it. And Jorgensen had the right idea. We'll use it, with variations. We'll call for volunteers—and vote on the men who want to step out for the good of the rest of us. The man who's found least valuable to the ship—he goes."

Gar hesitated. Then he nodded, looked at Brand. "It sounds fair enough to me."

"Yes; it's fair enough," Brand muttered. "All right; we'll do it that way. Call them forward, Varney."

The tall man stepped to the ship's communicating tube and gave the "General Attention" signal. Response came back swiftly in quick bursts of words from rapid voices.

The men trickled forward slowly in ones and twos. They lined up opposite Brand and Varney. "Big Lan" Margot, the chief compressor technician, boss of the bunch, with his shambling walk and hesitant grin, flashing like a gleam of light over his heavy dark face. De Celle, the French Earthman, thin and quick and sharp, like a polished rapier bending and straightening and casting off sparks of direct glow. Su Gan, the small Moon native, half terrestrial in his parentage, and showing the best alchemy of mixed blood—a little man, fast on curved feet, eager to please, glad to work, with a birdlike glitter in round eyes. Eight of them, filing in, crowding the small room, standing uneasily against the wall, wedged in between the control board and the televise panel, staring with grimy, uncertain faces at the glimmering cluster of reflected glow shown on the screen.

Jorgensen came in last, moving up the machine-room ladder with slow deliberation. He took his place near the televiser, his thin-eyed glance tightly focusing on Brand's body.

Brand faced them. "Jorgensen's told you by now what we're stacked against. I'm not wasting words with you. You're men, not children. You've got nerve or you wouldn't be here. You knew you'd have to fight when you came on this voyage. What I've got to offer is fair to all of us, from myself to Jorgensen."

Jorgensen nodded, suddenly spoke: "You're going to ask for a man with nerve enough to go out through the E lock, aren't you, sir?"

Brand hit him with direct eyes. "That's what I was trying to say. I'd like any of you who, of your own will, are ready to go out through the emergency port—to take one step toward me."

Margot shuffled forward. De Celle was a unit with him, in a quick skipping jump. Su Gan sidled across the smooth floor on lithe feet. Jorgensen walked even with them, still using that slow deliberation in the way he carried his body, as if he held a sense of successful purpose exulting within him.

Brand looked them all over again. Every man of the crew stood in an even line stretching across the silent room. Brand felt his eyes smart with moisture, and it was not all due to the bad air.

His voice snapped hoarsely: "I'd counted on this. That makes all of us, myself and Varney and Gar having already decided, who are willing to step out—for the good of the ship. We've hit upon this idea to settle it: we'll take a vote, and the man voted least valuable to the cause as a man and as a leader—will go. You agree?"

"There's no need for that," Jorgensen said softly. He took another step toward Brand; and then, turning, he swung on the men who remained in line.

"We don't have too much time," Jorgensen said with composure, "No good wastin' part of it takin' a vote. It's me that's dropping out through the lock."

There was a period of silence. None of the men objected. A slow smile twisted the little man's lips, as if he was watching himself from a point of observance in the far distance; listening to the faint irony of his words, and laughing without bitterness at his fine play acting. Only it was not play acting. It was real. Little Jorgensen was going out through the side port—for the good of the ship.

Varney put his eyes on the small man's silent face. "You want to do it that badly?"

"I've read stories from the recording spools on Earth," Jorgensen said, "and I'm trying to prove you don't have to be big to be a hero. I want to know what the taste of glory is like to have in your mouth."

Gar moved as if in protest, and Brand's eyes tightened in narrow lines, but Varney went to Jorgensen and they began working together coolly. With quick leaping jerks of his long hands over his body the small man was stripping himself, sliding into the cool embrace of a metal-armored space suit, then motioning to Varney to get at the mechanism of the emergency lock.

Finally he stood at the edge of the inner panel of the port, the face plate of the suit opened for the entrance of death. He turned his eyes once around the room, stopping his glance on Brand and Gar. He laughed a little, the sound echoing hollowly from within his clumsy suit.

He called over to them: "This is a great thing I'm doing, isn't it?"

Brand didn't answer.

But Varney grinned. "Yes; you'll be a hero of the cause."

"After I'm dead," Jorgensen agreed and laughed.

"After you're dead."

None of them heard what Jorgensen said next, except Varney. Varney wasn't sure he heard it, either. But he thought Jorgensen whispered:

"I'm glad to do this thing. You know, it's only right I should be doing it—I'm really a Bottom Level man—"

Then Jorgensen took a big breath and said quickly: "Never think it wasn't worth it, will you? All right, I'm ready."

Varney spun the dials feverishly, his damp hands slipping on the knobs of the smooth metal.

Brand came out of his daze, ran across the room, shouting in protest: "Can't let him do this! No, stop—"

He was at the lock, pushed Varney away, Gar following close behind. Varney stood staring at both of them, something sardonic in the twist of his thin mouth.

"You're a little bit late to stop the party," Varney said. "He just passed out."

V.

Above the sound of Varney's cold laughter, they heard the swift puff and burst of outward leaping air, as the outer lock panel opened to Jorgensen's body. And after that—well, after that, no sound got through from the void into the control room.

"He had what you might call—insides," Varney said heavily. "He stepped right into it."

Gar was staring at the small look-out plate over the control board. His hand jerked around in a queer circling gesture.

"Come here, Rafe. You can see—what's left of him."

Brand came and stood beside Gar, and they strained their eyes together. Closely watching, they both saw it—the small armored body, still spinning behind the ship, turning over and over with the force of the outrushing air not yet spent. Some vagrant gleam of light, traveling aimlessly from Moon or stars or Sun, struck the metal suit, glittered brightly for an instant, showed them a vision of Jorgensen's face, tucked inside the helmet.

He had left the face plate open, as they remembered. His eyes, bigger than they had been in life, as if death had been astounding, were shut, tightly closed by covering lids, as if at the final instant he had been unwilling to look out at the void into which he was mercilessly driven—but there was no fear frozen into the calm lineaments of the fading face.

There was something scarlet around his lips and eyes, like the red fringe around a Spanish shawl—blood it must have been, from burst vessels and ruptured veins, wrenched by the sudden removal of air pressure normal to an Earth-woven body; but still again there was no great change, not as much as Brand had believed there would be. He seemed simply to writhe in disturbed sleep.

The indifferent sliver of light, having been reflected from the little armored body to the eyes of the watchers, dwindled as Jorgensen dwindled, until finally they both vanished, leaving the steady lanterns in the sky which had always been there—the unchanging stars. Jorgensen, little Jorgensen of the Bottom Levels of Earth, was buried in the black shroud of space.

Brand spoke harshly, breath pounding his throat: "The most horrible death any man could have. And we sent him to it—"

"You really think it is so horrible?" Gar said quietly, still staring, oddly fascinated. "I don't agree. He looked pretty peaceful."

"I thought that, too," Varney said. "Oh, I don't suppose it was so bad."

Brand looked sharply at them both and swung away. He passed a hand across his face, rubbed his eyes hard, shook himself, and slid down into the seat in front of the control panel.

"Send the men aft," Brand muttered. "We've got to get moving faster. Varney, how much air reserve have we? I mean the stored oxygen we put aboard in emergency supplies—for use in case the compensator failed? The compensators are gone now; you'd better get to using that reserve."

"Right," Varney agreed and nodded. "I think we've got enough to carry us to Tycho—with one less man. And if we can pull away from the Controls—"

"I'm trying that last now," Brand said grimly, hands working at the great board. He sent out an attention call to the aft-compressor room.

Margot, the chief technician, rumbled an answer.

"You giving us all you've got back there?" Brand demanded. Silence.

Then Margot said hesitantly: "I might do a little better, chief, if we cut down on lights and gravity in the grids—and if you're willing to take the chance on blowing the fire coils."

"We'll take that chance," Brand said. "Jorgensen took a bigger one."

Margot stiffened. "Yes, sir."

For a little while after the other had cut off, there was no change.

Then speed came into the dials before Brand. Black needles trembled on pressure gauges, shifted far over toward the limit of the dial, edging past the red tracery of the danger point; the dark fingers of the acceleration indicators began to feel the purring flow of power, climb upward. Still the fleet of the Controls came on, kept creeping closer. Gar and Varney watched the clustered ships behind grow larger on the televisor screen, take shape and solid outline, strengthen into entities separate and distinct, in place of blurred blobs of distant light. Brand muttered softly, stabbed his hands against the green handles of the master switches in a sudden frenzy.

Varney asked: "Still gaining?"

Brand answered in one clipped breath: "Still gaining. Oh, if I could have a little more power!"

Gar's voice came: "We could cut off this big screen you and I are using, Varney, and keep track of the Controls from Brand's lookout plate. Would that help?"

"Yes," Varney muttered.

"Help?" Brand echoed. "It'll help plenty. Got any more ideas like that, Gar?"

"One more, and then I'm afraid I'm through."

"Well, let's hear the one you've got."

"Right!" Gar said. "Cut off all gravity from the grids. Under this acceleration, we'll scarcely miss it, and the grids eat a little power, don't they?"

Brand nodded. "Sure, they do. While I'm connecting with Margot to tell him that, Varney can block out that screen. O.K.?"

"Yes," Varney said.

He leaned forward, changed the set-up of tubes and condensers, snapped a switch, disconnected circuited wiring. The huge screen dimmed, faded, grew dark. Gar nodded, moved across the room to Brand's position, stood behind the other, watching. Varney followed silently. Standing side by side, they were both suddenly very still.

Brand muttered: "Close!"

"But it's not enough?" Varney asked heavily.

Brand's eyes flickered. "No. It's not enough."

Gar spoke, not looking at Varney: "How much more will it take to put us over?"

"Don't know exactly," Brand said. "But only a little more, and we'd be clear—with the lead we've piled up in three days."

"Then they've stopped gaining?" Gar asked eagerly.

Brand snarled at him without patience. "No! They're still coming up on us, but we've shaved down the difference in speed. Their lead ship is making three thousand even; and the *Isis* is sticking just above twenty-eight hundred—"

"How much of a lead have we got?" Varney demanded.

Brand hesitated an instant, glancing at dials, calculating fast. "Around twenty-five thousand miles. And we're losing that."

Decision came in his eyes. He snapped the attention call again; got the chief technician growling at the other end of the connection. Then he said: "You've taken out all the stuff you were using for gravity?"

"Yes, sir."

"Then tone down on heat and air circulation. And anything

else you can think of. We've got to have every atom of power you can scrape together. Understand that?"

"Yes, sir."

"Break."

Margot broke communication.

Brand looked at the two standing behind him. "Listen," he said. "We're in for a taste of cold for a while—and some other things. We're none of us going to be very comfortable, but we'll do the best we can. Get in those seats and strap yourselves—tight."

Varney obeyed in slow silence; but Gar clung to the back of Brand's place in a tightened grip, waved the other away.

"I'll stick here a little longer," he said. "As long as I can hold out. I might help, some way."

Brand shrugged. "All right. But watch yourself." Gar caught at that thought. Help the ship, some way. If there was only something he could do. There *was* something he could do, something he had to do. He had known it for a long time. Might as well admit it now, no use hiding it from himself— he'd been afraid, he had let Jorgensen—

He loosened his hold on the rounded ege of the control chair, took careful steps across the room to where Varney sat strapped in, each movement lifting his thin body high off the floor grids, to come drifting down again in a slow float. Queer sensation, that was. No gravity in the grids, nothing to hold you back, pull you down; a feeling of exultance went through you, walking like this—smooth power flowed through your muscles, you glided with light easiness.

He touched Varney on the shoulder.

Varney said, not moving his mouth: "What are you trying to do?"

"Don't you know?" Gar said, staring straight into his face.

Varney dropped his eyes. "No."

"It's just my job," Gar said simply. "I tried to shift if off on Jorgensen's shoulders, but I didn't get by. I'm glad I've got the chance to make up for that in the only way I can."

"Sit down here," Varney said, not answering him. "I'll strap you to this seat next to me."

"You're listening," Gar said, "and I know it. I let Jorgensen go, because I was afraid. And because I didn't believe in this thing as much as he did. I thought what Brand thought and you thought—for centuries some men have been trying to do something for the bottom of the pyramid. None of them, so far, have succeeded very greatly. And I thought it wasn't worth dying for. But it was—little Jorgensen showed me that it was."

Varney said: "Maybe you're right. But what can you do, now? He's gone. He dropped out, and it didn't do us any good. What are you going to do now?"

"I'm using power," Gar said softly. "Every time I breathe, I use a little power, I'm holding the ship back a little I haven't got weight, with the gravity gone, but I've got mass. I'm a drag pulling the ship down. So I'm going to stop breathing. I'm going to leave the ship."

"You're out of your head," Varney said. "Jorgensen went that way; one is enough. We'll get clear without any more of that."

Gar stood there, swaying a little on his uncertain feet. "No use lying, Varney. We both know the truth. You were thinking of dropping off yourself."

The other's eyes changed. "No. I wasn't. That's what bites into me. I wouldn't have the nerve. I'm scared."

"So am I," Gar said softly. "But you'll help me, won't you?"

A curtain of silence stretched between them. Brand was muttering again at the controls, his voice disjointed and incoherent, a heavy murmur creeping out across the room. Gar waited.

Varney made a harsh sound in his throat and looked once at Brand's curved back. Then he nodded and began to fumble with numb fingers at the straps binding him in.

"If you want to go," Varney muttered. "I guess I can't stop you." He jerked upward out of his seat, rose high, touched the room's ceiling with his shoulders, dropped at a long sloping angle to the floor. Brand heard the thud of that light fall and swiftly turned.

"What're you two doing?" Brand asked.

His glance shifted to the space suit, sprawling in an ungainly awkwardness on the floor near the E lock. Then he knew.

Gar stood silent a while. Then he said: "I'm doing what I

should have done, before Jorgensen dropped out. He gave me back my nerve. It's my job. He tried, but he couldn't do it for me. Maybe what I'm going to do will give the chance to you and Varney to get through. You've got the ship to work clear, and the two of you can do it. That's your job."

Brand didn't speak for a long space. He sat still, meeting Gar's steady eyes, listening to the other's words. Then he moved. "Varney," he said. "Take over here. I'll handle Gar. If anybody else goes—"

"It won't be you," Gar said flatly.

Varney stood hesitant.

Brand roared: "You got what I said! Take over."

Varney took over.

Brand glanced at him once, and stood beside Gar. "I'm not letting you do this," he said quietly. "Understand that?"

Gar took a slow shuffling step toward the E lock. Bending down, he lifted the heavy metal-fabric suit with both hands, held it out.

"Hold the suit while I strip," Gar said. He grinned. "Funny—I'm going out the same way I came in, wearing skin over bones."

Brand's legs shook. He turned his head, hands still at his sides. "Gar, you've got nerve."

"Nerve?" the other muttered. "Maybe. Maybe I have. Hold this suit."

"All right!" Brand said, the trembling burned out of his voice.

He stood the suit up on the stiff metal legs, then held it with steady fingers, even helped the other slide slowly down into its metal embrace. There came to him the power to fit the helmet close in the neck groove, lock mesh slips fast, give Gar one last steady look through the open face plate.

"All set?" he asked.

"All set!" Gar said.

Brand found it possible to be proud. His fingers plunged at the mechanism of the inner lock. The smooth panel moved back, merged into a narrow opening. Opening into space—Gar came close, brushed across Brand's body, felt the other touch against him, and stood head down inside the lock.

The trembling shook Brand's legs again for a long instant.

He stumbled, swayed against the closing switch, flung it over in a quick convulsive jerk. The inside panel snapped shut.

"Now," he muttered softly.

His fingers flashed up again, spun the gimbaled control that released the outer plate, sent air and man spinning in headlong flight from the lock. He heard the gushing whine of gas expanding into free space, caught the scrape of a metal body against the ship's side. He straightened, eyes dim. Gar was gone.

VI.

Brand went across slowly to where Varney worked with feverish fingers, body crouched, face bent over the lighted mechanism of the power board, head twisted away. He touched Varney. Varney looked up, eyes squeezed in painful pin points.

"He dropped out?"

"Yes," Brand said. "All through—all through!"

Varney hesitated, respecting the meaning of his sudden silence. Brand remained staring at the vision plate inset above the controls, his eyes fixed on a glinting point of light—light reflected brightly for a time from the spinning metal body drifting back through the space behind the ship. Brand shook himself, rubbed a harsh hand across his face. He looked at his fingers in the dim light. Moisture there. Shouldn't be. Sweat. No. Not sweat—but his face was for some reason a little damp.

He glanced up again, and saw the clustered glow that held the center of the visa plate. The antagonism within him was intensified into flame; he felt a terrible hate for the ships behind.

"Varney, how much lead—now?"

Varney calculated swiftly, fingers flying. "Twenty thousand."

Brand caught his breath. "Twenty thousand! Speed?"

Varney stared, his eyes frozen on the steady dials of the banked board before him. Then he swung around, exultance throbbing in swift words: "Speed approaching three thousand!"

Brand cried out hoarsely: "Then soon they'll stop gaining! And we've a lead of twenty thousand!"

He sucked wind into his lungs. "Say, we're pulling clear!"

"It looks like it," Varney said, grinning. Then his smile was wiped off his face.

Brand looked at him. They both held the same thought and knew it.

Brand asked, softly: "Varney, when did we cross twenty-nine hundred?"

Varney's glance shifted.

"Tell me," Brand said in a fierce voice. "You've got to tell me. And don't try to lie."

Varney knew what the other meant. He said: "Just before Gar went out."

"Before!" Brand groaned.

He stiffened and stood up straighter, hands gripping the edge of the control seat. "Before Gar went out—Then what he did wasn't necessary. We could have gone through without having him—you've checked on that?"

Varney steadily faced him. "I've got it down here, tabulated. But you've forgotten something. Twenty-nine hundred wouldn't be enough. We needed three thousand. And we've got it. Gar put us over. We'll cut across just in front of that meteorite cluster, holding three thousand even, and the patrol ships will hit the thick of it. When that happens, they've lost us, and they'll know it. They'll turn back."

Brand nodded dimly, as if no more than half comprehending. He moved his head, then his eyes took on a bitter keenness again. "All right; I'll take over. Are we close enough to start calling 17, Tycho?"

Varney nodded. "Think so. You mean, then—we're going to keep on fighting?"

Brand said: "Why ask a damn fool question like that? Didn't—wasn't that what Gar wanted?"

Life was in Varney's face again, a spark lighted his bleak eyes. "Yes. Gar—and Jorgensen."

"And Jorgensen," Brand said softly.

He was watching the glimmering square of the televisor reception plate. It was beginning to pulse and flicker, as if jerking to the impact of a tight short-wave beam, reaching out across blank space to the speeding ship.

Brand expelled a sudden swift cry of triumph. He moved his fingers in a rapid, intricate tracery. The screen shifted, gave a short vision of the looming face of the giant Moon, showed a stabbing flash of light leap up and die in a lunar crater, faded and came again. Then the beam plunged deeper through infinity, changed to detail, caught the outline of a bleak sending transmission room, with a tall man working at the controls of a high-power televisor. The man nodded and grinned, feeling the contact, and gave a swift salute.

"Crater 17, calling the *Isis*!"

"Contact made!" Brand cried.

"Contact made!"

Varney made a strangled sound of joy, gripped Brand hard. Brand half turned, then swung back, built up closer connection with the distant sender.

The snap faded from the captain's voice; abruptly he looked over his shoulder at Varney, muttered: "Take over again."

Varney nodded, helped Brand up from the narrow seat, then buckled himself in, and sent a call to the machine room for gravity to be poured again into the grids. Margot stolidly took the order and agreed.

Varney, on impulse, swung the light beam away from the crater near Tycho, sent it back along the ship's arc to the dimming blur of confused light that was the Controls' fleet; dark objects, great jagged groups of iron and stone, swept in between the *Isis* and the pursuing fleet, blotted out the savage ships. Varney's lip curled in a vindictive grin at the sight of the sudden scurry of movement in the patrol.

"I hope they break their damned necks!" he muttered then jerked at the dials before him, fingered out again for contact with the crater transmitter—Got it!"

"Crater 17, calling the *Isis*! Why don't you answer? Why don't you answer? Contact broken."

"Contact made," Varney said, grinning. "Got you the first time."

"Is this the *Isis* again?"

"Right!"

The other flashed: "Did you have trouble coming over?"

Varney's lips laced. "Yes. Bad trouble. Everything wrong on

Earth. Gagin sold out."

The answer came: "We know. Controls have had patrol ships sweeping Tycho for three days back. But we didn't get the whole set-up here. We are waiting for orders."

Varney swung. "Brand, you heard that? What'll I give them?"

Brand was looking back through spurned space, eyes straining for a last glimpse of a spinning metal body. He straightened, came over.

"Brand talking. Give you plenty of orders when we berth there. Have the A-cradle ready, and we'll use it shortly. I'm bringing the *Isis* straight in."

The distant operator nodded. "Right, chief! We'll be ready."

"And we're coming," Brand said harshly. "Break!"

The connection faded. Varney sat staring, face blank, fingers relaxed and numb, touching the cool metal of the huge directing panel.

He glanced away, followed Brand's eyes out through space: "They've beaten us."

"This time," Brand said savagely. "But we're going to fight again."

Far behind them indifferent splinters of light struck for an instant on the shapeless blob of a metal-fabric space suit—and went on to blaze in blurred brightness against the sides of shining ships, the patrol fleet, turning back toward Earth.

Star Ship Invincible

A novelette of courage and fear, beauty and horror and pathos—evoked by the dread, unfathomable menace of the "sink hole of space."

I.

HE had been sitting hunched on the high stool of the operator's chair, elbows on the smooth ledge of metal that encircled him, when the receptor tube spat a harsh wound in his ears, a sibilant warning note. He thought, "What now!" but straightened with alacrity, his stiff back shaping a tense angle.

He jerked his head upward in an arc, nostrils widened, his thin nose slightly trembling, as if he could smell what was vibrating through the receptor channel. He forgot how cold he was, and how his stomach ached faintly from many days on a diet of compressed-food tablets, and how he wished his relief would come, because he was lonely, the universe seeming strange and hostile all around him.

He could see too many stars from this round room that bulged in a curve outward from the top of the Jupiter Dome. It was not good for a man to see too many stars too long.

The snapping sound cracked like a whip in his ears again, and a voice roared: "G-16, the Dome!"

"Jupiter Station," he said quietly. "G-16 responding. Graham at the key. Ready."

The hard voice rumbled: "Build for visual projection. S 1. Jan Garth will speak to you."

"Standing by," Graham said. "R tube clear. Projection

coming—what channel?"

"A-channel," the voice boomed. "Beam Central, Earth, sending. Set up cross waves for head and shoulders. Use tight beam on a reverse arc."

"Power?" he asked faintly. "We're low here. The supply ship you were going to send—"

"All the power you've got," the voice cut in, brusque and commanding.

"Right," Graham muttered.

His hands, supple in metal-fabric gloves, caressed the complex panels in front of him as if he were playing a delicate musical instrument. He kicked a lever attached to one leg of his stool and the tripod chair began to revolve, slowly and smoothly.

As he turned he touched studs. The power tubes that ringed him in concentric rows hummed and howled, then went achingly silent, as the pulsating tight beam passed the wave band of audible reception.

His eardrums hurt: there had been a soundless concussion, and a golden sphere, slightly flattened at the ends, had come into being directly over his head. It hung suspended between the four great mirrors over him, spraying his face with lances of swirling light. He worked his lithe hands, fast.

A blue luminosity grew from his keyboard, spurted upward from the power tubes, forming like sapphire frost on levers and studs. Azure spears pushed at the glowing globe. His fingers danced over the power panels. The globe was held in balanced suspension in a basket network of crossing rays. It turned on an invisible axis, revolving with silent speed. Spinning like a dervish, the head and shoulders of a big man shaped within the hazy edges of the illuminated sphere.

Graham turned his twitching face upward. He whispered to himself, a little queerly: "Nice trick. You do it with mirrors."

He wanted to laugh—or cry. Sweat lay in heavy drops between his fingers. Visual projection always seemed like magic to him.

After all he was only a flabby little man who knew the motions, the incantations, that brought this magic into being. He handled forces he was terribly afraid of within himself. He was always wondering why the chained lightning in the tubes didn't turn and rend him; he thought some day it would refuse to perform its tricks, would swing and destroy him in a sudden burst of coldly coruscating flame.

The gleaming globe still whirled above him, but the spinning slowed, as he narrowed the flow of juice pouring into the A-channel. There were manacled giants in the tubes, but he could make them weak by starving them, by throttling the leaping flow of power that fed them.

The image in the sphere was at first vague and seemed to be upside down. Then the head and shoulders of the projected vision came right side around, the shape of face and neck clarifying first, then the line of lips and jaw slowly sharpening and straightening. Presently Graham had no difficulty at all in recognizing the grim countenance of Jan Garth, Administrator of Star Lines.

"Jupiter supply ship left Mars this date, 12:40, Mars time reckoned in Earth units," Garth said abruptly. "Watched the blast-off through my v-plate here. Record the time for permanent preservation."

"Recorded," Graham said, very low. He had taken it on the absorbent tape.

As soon as adequate projection had been built up, he had switched in the recording spool. Garth didn't say anything for half a minute after that terse exchange of crisp phrases. It was the first time the administrator had used the Jupiter beam personally, and for an instant the harsh voice stumbled, as if the man speaking had suddenly been brought up against reality in his mind; as if he had just awakened to what he was really doing.

He was talking—no; an image of himself was talking—in a little room high up under the roof of the interplanetary dome on Jupiter, a room separated from where he stood on Earth by an immensity so vast that the thought of it stunned a man into somber silence.

At last Garth said: "The ship is one of ours. Registered at the Port of Korna, nine thousand tons Earth weight; carrying pilot, navigator, and twenty-eight passengers. The *Star Ship Invincible*. Captain Moran commanding."

"New ship," Graham said succinctly.

"Maiden voyage. It's the first of the new fleet."

"Carrying supplies for the Dome here?"

"Yes."

"We need plenty," Graham said, biting his words.

He shivered, suddenly realizing that he was very cold. Jupiter's atmosphere didn't hold heat, the Sun was very far away; and they had only a little more fuel to feed into the atomic converters. Until the supply ship came, the Dome would be cold.

"I know," Garth said.

"Why did you wait so long to send this ship?" Graham demanded recklessly.

He forgot the power of the other; he forgot that he was only Key Man G-16, Jupiter Station; he thought of how they had to live, here in the Dome, sleeping restlessly in chilly cells, groping through corridors kept dim because light took power and you didn't mind not seeing very well if you could stay at least partially warm. And always the faint ache in their bellies; the ache that came from month after month on the same diet of compressed synthe-food.

Garth said: "This is only a little later than usual. The ship will be there soon. Hold hard."

Graham hunched his shoulders. "You—you haven't forgotten the Sink Hole?"

Garth said: "No."

"The ship's carrying passengers?"

"Yes. Twenty-eight."

"They've been warned?"

"They've been warned."

Graham nodded. "Well, Moran and his navigator know what to expect."

"They're not going to have any trouble."

"You're pretty sure," Graham said softly. "This ship—she's fast?"

The big man shifted his head, raising it with exultance. "I told you; it's the first of the new fleet we've been building on Mars for the Jupiter run. Since the Sink Hole came, we've been working night and day. Now we're ready to take a chance."

The little man sat still, his body humped, feeling the sweat gather in the cold palms of his hands. They were taking a chance, were they? This new ship must be big stuff; at least the lab men thought it was big stuff.

A picture rose in his brain. He glimpsed strained faces, looked into the worried yet courageous eyes of the passengers—passengers who were, he knew, friends and lovers of the people already here in the Dome. They knew what might happen, those passengers; yet they went aboard the *Star Ship Invincible* because the touch of a friendly hand, the pressure of lips and bodies in the physical contact of love, meant more to them than living a safe existence full of the emptiness of fading memories.

They were coming unafraid, risking everything, knowing that the Sink Hole might never close again; because it had closed once before, after an interval of ten yawning years, was no guarantee that it would close now after this reopening. They came, knowing they might be put away forever from the good Earth.

They weren't willing to be cut off from the other planets for ten years, waiting for the Sink Hole to shut together in its periodic pulsation. Ten years was a long time; too long, these faithful ones believed, too long for separation. So they risked more than life for—

"You're not taking the big chance," Graham said after a minute. "Those people aboard the *Invincible* are doing that."

Garth shrugged, "People are always taking chances. That's life, isn't it—taking chances?"

Graham said: "I don't know. Maybe it is."

"They've got everything in their favor," Garth stated. "The Walton Arc is still clear. The Hole's widening slowly this time. And the ship has the speed to make port at the Dome, before the Hole spreads across the Walton Arc."

"I hope you're right," Graham muttered.

All at once a realization came to him, and he went cold in every part of his body. He thought: God, she may have decided to come this trip. Even now she may be on the *Invincible*, not knowing the danger, not sensing fully that the ship rides a race with death. The passenger list—the names of those who were coming on the *Invincible*. He had to know.

He tried to keep the shivering out of his voice, but it was there when he spoke: "You—you'd better let me have the names of the passengers, chief. The people here will want to know who's aboard that ship."

Garth looked at him closely. "All right; I'll give it to you. I've got the record here. Better take this on the tape."

"Yes, sir," Graham said, very low. "The names, sir?"

Garth's hand appeared in the projection, holding a strip of metal-fabric, stamped indelibly with a string of names and numbers; he began to read, his voice low, his eyes now and then glancing at the signal man's face; since the projection had been built on a tight beam operating along a double arc, Graham's body was visible to the man on Earth. The list wasn't long; only twenty-eight passengers. Almost the last in the roll was the name Graham had hoped and feared might be there. There couldn't be any doubt now. The girl had gone aboard the *Invincible*. It all depended now on Moran—on Moran and whatever they had developed in the experimental laboratories on Mars. This ship—there was something about the way Garth spoke of it that gave him hope.

"I've got them all," Graham said, as the harsh voice of the administrator faded out. "Thank you, sir."

Garth stared at him keenly. "Any one you know listed there?"

The little man stammered something incoherent.

"Can't hear you," Garth said, indifferent now. For a moment he had been amused by the taut anxiety that had crept into the key man's gaunt face, but after all it was nothing to him; he didn't care very much what answer the flabby fellow made.

"Only my wife," Graham said. He choked, and then went on: "Couldn't you tell me what this ship has that the others hadn't, sir? And what—what do you want me to do? There must be something I can do. If I could help to keep her safe it would mean so much to me."

"I understand." Garth softened for an instant; really, the fellow was quite human, with his pleading eyes and twitching little face. "Yes; there's something you can do. You'll connect with the *Invincible* immediately after I've signed off here. Once you've got them, you'll transfer the channel on relay to my operator here, but keep your own key open. Moran is under orders to use the automatic time signal, on a circuit breaker operating every other minute. So long as you hear that signal, you'll know the ship's all right."

"Sure," Graham said. "But suppose it fades?"

"If you think something's wrong, you'll flash my operator and report."

"That's all I've got to do?"

"That's all."

"It's not much," Graham whispered.

Garth turned. "There isn't much we can do if the *Invincible* goes under. I can't believe it will go under."

"Yes," Graham said eagerly. "You said it had a lot of new gadgets. You couldn't—couldn't tell me what they were?"

"It's the best ship we know how to build," Garth said slowly. "I'm not a lab man, so I don't know the jargon or the details, but it's got everything we could put into it. You needn't worry. Moran is the best pilot-commander we have, and Hansen's a navigator; they'll bring this ship through."

Graham shook his head, his lips trembling. "This thing won't be decided by navigating. It will depend on the ship—on speed, on power, on equipment."

Garth straightened, smiling a little. "Well, this vessel is named the *Invincible*."

Graham shivered. "Wrong name. I'm afraid of names like that."

The other threw back his big head and laughed. "Have you got any sensible reason for being afraid?"

"Yes," Graham said.

The heavy-faced man looked at him, suddenly grave. "You'll explain."

"Sure!" Graham said. "I—I've had a lot of time to read the old books here in the station. I mean the old printed books the ancients had before the tape recorder and the film spool. There's a story of a ship of the sea that was built about two hundred years ago, in the twentieth century—"

"Go on," Garth ordered.

"It struck an iceberg—there were icebergs on Earth then; this was before climate control—and it went down. Right under, in just a little while. About a thousand people were drowned, counting the passengers."

Garth shrugged. "What's that got to do with the ship we

built on Mars?"

"The experts said this ship of the sea wasn't sinkable," Graham said quietly. "Well, they were wrong. They seem to have found then that anything man could make could be easily destroyed. We've had to learn that lesson over and over."

After a silence Garth said: "What was the name of this sea ship?"

Graham answered: "They called it the *Titanic*."

Neither of them moved for a while.

Then Garth shouted: "But you don't know this ship that Moran is commanding. It's made of an alloy, the newest alloy we've yet found; tungsten isotope and C-metal. The hull is split in cylindrical sections twenty feet in diameter over all. The sections are honeycombed with cells; the cells are bulkheaded, shock-proofed, deadened with molecular insulation. The ship is armor-plated in three layers, with vacuum between each layer."

Graham kept thinking of the girl; and not of the girl alone, but of all of them on the *Invincible*; crouching in a little metal bubble that hurtled at inconceivable speed along the Walton Arc, along a plotted curve that passed just beyond the edge of the Hole in Space. Just beyond—maybe. If the Hole didn't grow. And the Hole was growing.

His throat was bitter and dry. "It's no good if you've been preparing against collision. The Hole isn't solid, isn't material or tangible. What the ship's got to have is power—power to pull away."

"You think," Garth said slowly, "the Hole is something like a vortex or a whirlpool? And when a ship comes too near it's sucked under."

"Now you've got it," Graham siad.

For a minute they both sat very still, staring at one another with opaque eyes; Graham could hear the sibilant singing of the discharge spark in the R tube behind him. He waited.

"The lab men have given the *Invincible* all the power we knew how to build into her," Garth muttered. "Etheric drive. If a ship's pulled into the Hole, it must come out somewhere. What's on the other side of the Hole?"

"We don't know," Graham said ironically. "I believe it lies

in a universe of different dimensional proportions; in a different kind of ether. Somehow that universe, or maybe it was our universe, warped a little out of line, and there's this gap where nothing fits. It begins and ends nowhere."

The other whispered: "The lab men developed an experimental shield—waves generated in a circular blanket that will cover the *Invincible* all over. So the ship can ride in a static ether."

Graham put up his hands suddenly and covered his gray face. "I wish I could feel that you'd gone about this right; that the lab men knew what they were building; but I can't be sure. All I can think about is my wife. We'd only been married a little while when I was transferred here. I didn't want to bring her out to this God-forsaken planet.

"The Hole opened and stayed open, for ten years. I haven't seen her in ten years. But I haven't forgotten. She has been faithful. I know that. Now she's coming to me on a ship that's got a good chance of falling into hell. Maybe I'll never see her again. Maybe I'll never feel her lips against mine again—"

The big man's eyes were hard and unyielding. "You'll see her soon. Don't be a damned fool. You've got a job to do. You can't go soft on me now. None of us can afford to go soft in this game. I couldn't recall the *Invincible* if I wanted to. The ship's gone too far along the Arc."

"No; Moran wouldn't turn back now," Graham said harshly. "I know him, the devil. He's hard as hell. He's like you. You've never been hit like I'm hit now. But wait—it's coming to you. Some day it's coming to you."

Garth laughed; the sound throbbed with immense contempt. This flabby little key man with the face of a rabbit shouting at him, talking like that to him! That was funny. Yes. Damned funny! He roared:

"If I gave the order, even now, Moran would turn back."

Graham grinned, peeling his lips back. "He's after glory. If he went on and made it through, he could laugh at you. He'd be a hero the system over. And if he didn't—what'd be the difference?"

Garth was stung. "You've got your orders, G-16. If the circuit breaker on the *Invincible* stops, you'll ring me in at once."

"Yes," Graham said. "Whatever Moran does, I'll obey orders, chief. I've been obeying orders all my life."

Garth muttered grimly: "You're not after glory, are you?"

"No. Moran can have that."

Garth grinned. "Cut off."

"Cutting off."

The opalescent sphere lost shape and the illusion of solidity; it dissolved like smoke, streaming away in banners of golden glow that vanished in a bright and glittering nothingness. It was gone and Graham sat alone. The stars closed in around him; millions of white orbs watching him. To them he must have been a queer specimen of tormented matter, convulsed by the strange madness called life, wriggling frantically away from the final transfixion that would be his destiny.

Shuddering, he pulled his thoughts from the stars. Before, he had been lonely, but not this lonely; now he ached with the completeness of his isolation. His belly was empty, and his heart was vacant, except for the hunger of a terrible longing; yet these things were as nothing to him. He sat staring down the long slope of fruitless years, seeing before him the shadow of coming bereavement. He felt now that the girl, his wife, still lived somewhere in space; but the warm pulsation of her unique being was burning low. Far away from him she brushed elbows unawares with death. Annihilation was nearer to her than she knew.

His longing and his loneliness, however, were not stronger in him than the lifelong habit of submission to command. Swinging in the chair he began to change the set-up of the power chart.

II

She stood at the foot of the burnished metal ladder that went up into the control cabin. Hesitantly, she caught her gleaming metal-fabric cloak about her and moved upward; halfway to the top she felt the ladder quiver under added weight, and, tilting her head, she saw a man coming rapidly down. He seemed to become conscious of her presence at the same time and stopped a little above her, staring.

He was a big man, the solid meat of his hard body revealed in muscular outline by the close fit of his space-man's uniform. Blond, burned by the light of suns and stars, he was handsome—an overpowering Nordic.

His lips twisted in a slow frown. "Do you feel the need of exercise, lady? I admit the ship's a little cramped back here, but still—climbing ladders—

She stammered something. Looking at her more closely and seeing that she was beautiful, his lips twisted a different way and he smiled.

"Didn't you know it's not allowed to go up into the control cabin?"

"Oh, yes," she said lightly. "I knew it." She returned his smile.

He said with a stumbling voice: "You're lovely, but at least you're not a lovely liar."

"Why should I lie?" she asked slowly. "I wasn't doing anything wrong. I was exploring the ship."

"I see," he said, very sober. "First voyage?"

"Almost," she said. "Except for the crossing I made with my father from Earth to Mars. I have no memory of that. I'm Earth-born."

"So am I," he said gently. "Then we'd better be friends. There aren't many Earth-born on this ship."

She nodded. Her burnished golden head moved with an easy grace. Eyes the color of starlit space looked upward into his. She said quietly:

"I've found that. I've had no one to talk to for nearly three days now."

"Hard on a woman," he said, grinning.

She laughed, delightfully.

He moved another rung downward on the ladder. "You've been lonely," he said. "I'm very sorry. Didn't know any one like you had come aboard—this trip. Should have looked at the passenger list more closely."

"You like me?" she whispered.

He put his head on one side, regarded her carefully, then answered, grave-voiced: "Yes. Definitely."

"I'm glad."

"All right," he said, with amusement. "Now, you like me?"

Her laughter tinkled. "Yes. Definitely."

He looked at her with a glow in his eyes. "I think," he said, "before this goes any further, we'd better get down from this ladder."

"I can't come up?"

"Persistent, aren't you?" he returned. "Sorry, but orders is orders, ma'am."

He laughed again. "Down with you, lady. Or have you a name?"

"I've a name," she said softly. "Tam. Tam Graham."

He felt a sudden keen pleasure in being alive. Three days of monotony, of watching charts and moving keys, hunched in a back-breaking crouch—three days full of overhanging terror were wiped away and he was glad he breathed and could see and smell and hear and taste. He tasted a word now, touching it tenderly with his tongue; the word was "Tam."

"Lovely," he said, without thinking. "It fits." So few people have the right names." She dropped down the ladder in a swift sinuous motion, and he followed her, closed his arms suddenly around her, and kissed the fragrant rosebud of her mouth.

"Some day soon," he said softly, "I'll take you up in the control cabin—if you're very nice to me."

He held his arms in the same tight circle, but somehow she slipped easily from his hold, and he stood empty-handed and a little stunned.

Gravely her smooth voice came: "I've a husband somewhere. You may have heard of him. John Graham."

He dropped his hands, the smile fell away from his lips, and his face was covered by a shadow; before this, he had considered himself as not without honor. He was somehow ashamed.

"Yes. Jupiter key man."

"I love him," she said simply. "I'm going to him."

"You're brave," he said. And then: "I'm sorry."

"Forgiven and forgotten," she said, now smiling. "I want you to be a friend to me. You're a friend of John's, aren't you?"

"G-16?" he said. "Oh, yes! My name is Hansen. I'm navigator, in case you didn't know."

"I knew," the girl said.

They looked at one another and laughed together, but the sound of his mirth was strained.

"You're wise. Too wise for me."

"In some ways, perhaps. About ships and space you know things that I shall never know. You're a navigator—that's hard. I've heard John say it was hard."

"Ordinarily," he said, eyes darkening, "it's pretty soft stuff. But not for me this trip. I wish we'd left you back on Mars!"

"Why?" she asked slowly.

"You're taking a long chance. It's fifty-fifty we'll never make Jupiter."

"There's danger," she whispered. "I know."

He glanced at her with admiration. "You have no fear. If you were afraid, I'd feel it. I can feel things like that."

She said softly: "You see, whatever comes, I'll always have the memory of the night we left Mars. The lights crossing in the sky, like pale fingers pointing. The lines of silver ships, and then this ship, a polished cylinder, lying in that immense trestlework—what do you call that?"

"Slip cradle," he answered, looking at her with glinting eyes. "It's the same with me. I remember every blast-off; even to the first trip I took as navigator, on the Mars-Earth run, five years ago. There's something about it."

"The thick Martian night," she said dreamily. "All those confused voices shouting. Monstrous machines and puny people. I'll never forget my first sight of those luminous letters on the side of this ship, stamped on the sleek curve of it: *Star Ship Invincible.*"

He nodded, his face strong with exultance. "*Invincible*—that's a proud name. Defiant!"

"Throwing back the light of the stars," Tam whispered. "As if to say—not afraid, not afraid, not afraid of what you can do to me. Not afraid of emptiness, of vastness, of the hard hostility written in the stars."

He shook his head. "The stars aren't hostile. They're indifferent."

"No," she said. "They hate us; I can sense it. They resent our arrogance, our impudence in voyaging out into the colossal sea of space where they have been so long alone."

He grinned. "They're only suns and planets; bright lights

along the Broadway of the universe."

"Suns and planets," she repeated softly. "And beyond them?"

He shrugged. "More suns and planets, I suppose."

"Forever and forever?"

"Forever, perhaps," he said, laughing.

"Worlds without end," she whispered, and shivered a little. "I feel small and insignificant. We won't talk of those things."

"All right," he said. They stood silent an instant, then he muttered:

"I suppose you've been all over the rest of the ship?"

"Yes," Tam answered. "I've been exploring. All those cold cells crowded with stellite drums and beryllium cylinders—they hold supplies?"

"That's it."

"For us? I didn't know we'd use so much."

He turned away from her, then swung back. "For us, and for the Dome on Jupiter. We'll use very little. This will be a short trip, if we make it. The ship has a new power source—etheric drive."

The girl looked at him soberly. "Now you talk of things incomprehensible to me. What is it, this etheric drive?"

"You remember your instructions in space school concerning three-dimensional calculations?" he asked. "Well, the drive is possible because we've gone back to the theory of an all-pervasive medium including the universe in its scope. By using a four-dimensional tesseract we are able to exert power directly on the ether.

"Think of the ether as a river in which we are completely immersed; by coming to the surface of the river we are able to ride a current and choose the direction of flow; the motions of the suns and planets are everlastingly stirring currents in the ether—ether drifts. They go in all directions, constantly crossing and recrossing one another. We've found a current Jupiter-bound, and we're riding it. All clear?"

The girl said, very low: "You mean, then, that at any time we may be hurled away from Jupiter instead of toward it if the drift changes direction?"

He frowned. "No. Naturally we've got a set of Donlin sun engines in reserve. And there's little chance of the direction of the ether flow changing. We can choose any drift we want and calculate its probable direction for twenty years to come. That is, we can do that by using the mechanical calculators. No man could think that fast—not even me. About all I do is feed the calculators problems. I think up the puzzles, they chew them up, and give me the predigested results."

The girl put one hand to her smooth forehead. "You've given me an ache—here."

He glanced at the little chronometer strapped to one wrist. "Well, you're going to be rid of me now for a while. I've got to back-track to the C cabin. Came aft to take a stroll through this part of the ship and see how things were going. Moran will expect some kind of a report. What shall I give him?"

"Tell him," the girl said, "all's well!"

"In more ways than one," Hansen muttered.

His mouth still burned with remembrance of that swift kiss. He was yet stunned with the knowledge that this was the wife of John Graham—this girl married to the flabby little key-man who had been for ten years marooned in the Dome. It wasn't easy to believe, because he didn't want to believe it.

The girl touched his arm timidly. "You'll come back again and talk to me?"

"Sure, I'll come back again. And maybe—I don't know, because Moran's a pretty sour old space-buster, but maybe, I say, I'll be able to take you up in the C cabin. I'll come again as soon as I can."

He made an exaggerated bow, kissed her hand, then smilingly turned away and vanished up the ladder. After he had gone, the girl raised her fingers and slowly rubbed them across her lips.

She went back slowly to the little cell in the ship's hull that had been given to her. It was no better, no worse, than the accommodations offered the other passengers. It was cramped and cold, but it was clean, almost Spartan in its austerity.

There was a wide bed, nearly level with the floor, the smooth silky surface of it shining softly. She sank down in the soft stuff, felt the warm fabric close around her, hold her in a firm yet tender embrace. She was tired with a weariness arising from monotony, yet no desire for sleep came to her.

She was lying very still, half dreaming, half waking, and it seemed only a part of the dream when a spot of yellow light appeared on the wall and a voice spoke to her with exultant eagerness: "Tam, I've found you!"

This was not dreaming. It was real. Too real. With a little gasp she answered, speaking wildly into the cone of saffron light that thickened and strengthened while she spoke:

"John—you can see me?"

His voice came, brokenly, the voice of a man given a rare vision: "Yes; I can see you. And you're beautiful. You're more beautiful than you were so long ago. The years have not changed you, nor time altered you, except to make you more wonderful."

She couldn't move, but her body shivered in a kind of ecstasy.

"This is like magic; like a miracle. John, where are you?"

"The Dome," he said faintly. "Jupiter."

"Let me see you," she said. "Darling, let me see you."

He didn't answer at once. Then: "This beam—works only one way. Hard to keep it narrowed on your cabin. No receiver at your end, no transmitter. Can't build a reverse arc."

She said softly: "It isn't possible?"

"No. It isn't possible."

She thought he seemed glad. That was strange. Yet it might have been only her imagining. She whispered:

"You've changed a little. Your voice is different."

He said: "Darling, I'm still the same, and you're still the same, and our love is as it has always been. And it will be the same through life everlasting."

"Ten years," she whispered. "A long time, John."

"Then you mean—well, I don't deserve you. And no woman could be faithful through ten years."

"But I have been faithful," she answered simply.

He would remember those words all his days.

"The ship," he said, after a silence. "Everything's all right?"

"Yes. In a little while I'll be with you."

His voice shook. "Darling, I can't wait. My arms have been empty so long."

"We waited ten years," she whispered softly. "The years are gone, and we shall not remember them. We have the hours that remain to us."

The shaft of vibrant light quivered and died away, leaving the room full of shadow and the echo of his exultant voice:

"Tam, you're coming to me!"

"Only a little longer," the girl cried to him. "Only a little longer, darling."

The light was gone and somehow a shadow lay over her heart. She had a sudden remembrance of the cold hostility she had seen written in the stars; and the ship still rode the sea of space.

III.

Hansen climbed the ladder into the control cube, feeling like an old man. His joints were stiff and bitterness was in his mouth. All his life he had waited for a woman like the one he had seen below; his eyes had been warmed by the vision of her, and the warmth had gone through his body, lighting torches in his veins. Now that flame was dead, abruptly quenched, and he was blinded by the pain of his spent longing.

He reached the end of the ladder and pulled himself up into the crowded room that had been his whole world during many hours of tense labor. His legs shook under him.

Captain Moran was standing in the middle of the cabin, looking at him.

"You've come back so soon?" Moran asked. "Why didn't you do as I said—take an empty cabin aft and sleep a while? You're very tired. So am I—but not so weary as you seem. Your face shows that, sir."

"Does it?" Hansen mumbled.

He rubbed an elbow against a slot in the wall and felt the smooth round surface of a sealing plug slip in place behind him. He stood an instant with his back against that cool metal stuff, unsmiling, his eyes on the dull gray of the floor.

"I can't sleep back there—with them."

Moran's lips tightened. "You mean, you're afraid the thing we're hoping won't happen, may happen, and you'd be caught with the passengers?"

"Hell, no!" Hansen said, his voice savage. "I'd rather take

my place with them than carry this knowledge around with me. They don't know they're doomed. When the thing happens to them, it will be sudden, sharp, complete, like an execution. They haven't been turning the possibility over and over in their minds, fighting the thought of it, then letting the thought sweep in and grow and grow, until it's like a monster devouring a man's thought-stuff. You and I have the joy of that."

Moran came closer to him, walking with tight, clipped steps. The captain put a hand on his shoulder.

"Nothing's gone wrong yet, Hansen. You're borrowing trouble."

Hansen's eyes flamed up at him. "Am I? Am I? So it hasn't been worrying you, eh? It hasn't been worrying you that we've the lives of twenty-eight people in our hands; that maybe we've got to let those twenty-eight people die, because we have our orders, and we obey—damned fools, we do what we're told, even when it comes to murder."

The older man didn't move for a minute. The hard, quiet face remained with that curious surface stillness all over it, the mask that had never fallen before Hansen or any other so far as he knew. Then Moran said:

"This isn't murder. They were warned, over and over. They came freely, knowing the chance they took. You and I would be glad to die with them. But we've got a different part to play—a harder part, maybe. I don't know about that. We're men. We'll behave as men."

Hansen straightened. He no longer needed the support of the cold metal slab against his back.

"Hell, you're right! But I—I've seen a woman; not an ordinary woman—she knocked me a little off balance. She seemed to me too beautiful to die. I wanted to save her. I couldn't breathe straight for a little while."

"Some women can do that to you," Moran said, understanding. "You've never taken a wife, have you? And it has come to you that this is the woman for whom you have waited."

"I know it," Hansen said very softly. "But it just couldn't be arranged. She's Tam Graham, G-16's wife, and she happens to love him."

Moran's eyes flickered. "Johnny Graham's wife! On this ship! I remember her. She is—beautiful. I can't forget the way he used to look at her. There's something between them like—like adoration. If anything happens to—"

"Yes," Hansen said. "No good thinking about it. We can't do anything for her. She's only one among many. There are other women riding with us—maybe not so beautiful physically, but beautiful with the same kind of love. It's the same with them as with Tam. It must be the same with them, or they wouldn't have taken this ship. They came with their eyes open. We can't save them all."

"No," Moran said. "You and I didn't make the Hole. We've got our job to do, and we'll do it, the best way we know how. The rest is on the knees of the gods."

Hansen nodded slowly. "Have you checked the chart since I left?"

"Twice," Moran said. "Speed's holding. We're on our course. We've got a good chance of pulling away clean."

They went over to the Danler spatial chart and stood staring at it together. A black smear, twisted like a snake, cutting across the smooth ivory luminosity of the board—that was the Sink Hole.

Swinging across the upper end of that ebony blur they could trace the faint red line of the Walton Arc. A green sliver of glow was the *Invincible*; the ship crawled deliberately, it seemed to them, along the scarlet curve. As it crawled, it came nearer and nearer the blob of unfolding darkness that was the Hole. It seemed as though some one had spilled ink on the white surface of the chart, and the ink was spreading, spreading—

Moran said; "We're doing better than Garth figured. I've balanced the chronometer readings with space-path calculations and made allowances for light distortions due to etheric faults, but still our speed is pretty nearly inconceivable."

"And if anything happens," Hansen said quietly, "we've still a trick in reserve. I don't understand how it's going to be done, but Garth gave you the directions."

"Listen," Moran said impatiently, "I explained it to you once. It's not simple, but you're a navigator with AA rating and dimensional mechanics should be understandable to you. Garth and the lab men believe the Hole is a dimensional warp. Using the etheric drive won't keep us from being pulled into it, or through it, or across it, if a vortex has been formed by the spatial strain caused by the opening of that gap in the void.

"All the etheric currents may be sucked one way, and we're riding an etheric current, you know. If the current we're on goes in the ship goes in. We're hoping against that. We're counting on the strength of the ether stream we're skimming now; we believe this flow will carry us by the Hole before it has fully widened across the Walton Arc. But we may be wrong."

Hansen grinned without mirth. "That's funny. You sound like an expert—'we *may* be wrong.' Hell, it's an odds-on chance the whole damned thing is cockeyed. I don't trust those lab men. Sure—they think up something like this, and then they stay where *they're* safe enough, but they send us space-wranglers out to try it on the dog. If it doesn't work right—that's too bad. Write it off. Unsuccessful experiment. They make a hell of a lot of unsuccessful experiments."

"That the only way science gets anywhere," Moran said heavily. "Trying and trying and trying. This is a swell ship we've got here, isn't it? It's pretty comfortable, it's clean, it's warm, we've got as good air to breathe as you'll find on any planet, we've got speed and power to burn—not much like the old space boats that used to creep out to the Moon from Earth and then crawl back. There have been improvements; we owe them to the lab men. We owe a lot to the lab men. We've got to take our chances, sure, but they're doing the best they can to make things easier and safer for us.

"Most of them would rather lock the doors of the laboratories and never come out again; they've got what they think is the holy of holies, and the world, our world, the practical world, the world of men and money and machines, is just a damned nuisance to them. We're a lot of childish creatures always begging for new toys, new gadgets, new playthings. We build a civilization, then tear it down, building something different. We don't know what we want."

"I know what I want," Hansen muttered. His fingers twitched. "I want to get this damned ship safe into the Dome at Jupiter, and then I never want to see another damned space-buster again as long as I live. I'm sick of seeing stars; I've got a bellyful of monotony without end."

"You're tired," Moran said. "You've taken too long a trick at the controls. I've felt the same way; world-weariness born of physical weariness. Why don't you trust the automatic pilot when you're on duty? Machines are better than men—for most things."

Hansen swung around, his face contorted. "Damn you, you're not human! You'd rather look at the shine of a stellite stud than see a smile break on a woman's face. You're all wheels and levers and clicking cogs; sometimes I expect to hear a humming and buzzing come from inside you."

Moran laughed with metallic amusement. "I can depend on machines. When you need them, they're there. This ship is a machine. The thing that may save you and me from going in the Hole with the rest of them—that's a machine, too."

"I don't know," Hansen grunted, staring at it. "Maybe it is; sometimes I think it's alive. It's a damned funny-looking thing."

Moran looked across at the dimensional converter with a kind of loving reverence. Smiling, he said: "It's beautiful. Notice! Not a wheel anywhere. That's why you can't believe it is a machine."

The converter was oddly like a flower—a flame flower with metal petals of vivid blue, and a purple cylindrical stalk luminous with an unceasing sweat of cold translucent bubbles that sifted out through a network of tiny apertures on the underside of the petals and flowed downward in a singing stream. It seemed to be covered by a shimmering veil of something shining and smooth and transparent like glass, yet not glass.

Moran whispered: "Try to follow the lines of it with your eyes. You can't. They seem to begin and end nowhere. Yet they have beginnings and endings—not in our universe, not in our dimensional range, but somewhere; somewhere beyond or around or over or under our world. When I think that our laboratory men shaped that mechanism, prisoned free power in it, and gave control of that power to the little cube in the wall there, I'm proud. I'm glad I'm a man. We're only crawling scum maybe, lice infesting the surfaces of dying planets—but by Heaven, we've got a few brains."

Hansen shivered. "I don't like it."

The other laughed. "You're afraid of it, because it's so beautiful and terrible."

"Yes," Hansen said, "I am." Then: "Well, what does the damned thing do?"

"When the time comes that we have to use it," Moran said, "you'll see. I'm trying now to tell you how it works. They've called it a dimensional converter, and that's the right name for it. When I touch that cube in the wall, it will swing, and the angles of its planes one to another will be reversed, and the shape of this room and everything in this room, including your body and my body, will be converted across the dimensions—just for an instant, a fragment of a second, we shall be nowhere. We shall still be in this ship and at the same time we shall be in a million otherwheres.

"There is only one dimension—shape. When we talk about length and width and thickness and existence in relative time, we are only attempting to describe shape. And not even that—what we are really doing is describing size. Size is real, is physical, is solid and touchable. But shape—how can you get hold of that and describe it?

"Shape is the estimation of a thing that we form from the physical and mental impressions and perceptions, sensations and stimulations, that impinge on our receptive mechanisms. We know how a thing looks, but we can't describe it; we can describe some of its physical aspects, and make a few fumbling comparisons with other inadequately described things, and finally we conclude with the generality that everything is relative. This converter is like reality—beautifully incomplete."

"Still what you've said isn't clear to me," Hansen muttered, moving his hands protestingly. "I can't get all this straight in my head. Where the hell will we go when this thing starts working on us—and where will we arrive?"

"We'll come back as nearly as possible to where we were," Moran said, grave-voiced. "Maybe that will be somewhere within the shell of this ship—if the ship exists after passing through the Hole."

His cold glance swung to the spatial chart. The green blob had moved forward: nearly half of the red line had been eaten away, but the arc that remained was very near to the ebony blur of the dead spot. The Hole was widening like a hungry mouth—

Moran nodded toward the space-drive dial. He said, with a kind of savage confidence: "Speed still the same. Course all even. We're not going to have any trouble."

"No," Hansen said. "No; of course not." He looked at the gray metal of the floor. "But I think I'll sleep here. It'll be better if we don't unseal that plug again until we reach Jupiter."

"All right," Moran said, bending over the chart.

Hansen stared at him; absorbed, intent on graphs and dial readings, he seemed indifferent to the existence of human weaknesses, human emotions. With him there could never be a great love. And yet—it might be that he loved his machines with a cold intellectual passion.

Hansen couldn't help shivering. He was thinking of the girl; all that beauty obliterated, sucked into nothingness, destroyed by a devouring darkness. It couldn't be. He couldn't let it be.

Muttering a little to himself, he put his hands up to his head. Looking at Moran's stiff back, he whispered:

"I'm going to do something. I can't let her die without doing something. I can't—"

Moran swung. "Did you speak to me?"

"No," Hansen said in a mumble. "I didn't say anything."

"Thought I heard you talking."

Hansen grinned queerly. "Now you're getting the jitters. Maybe you got 'em from me."

Moran frowned. "You'd better take a little sleep while you've got the chance. I'll be needing some myself pretty soon and it'll be your trick again; you'll want to be in good shape, if you're not going to use the automatic pilot."

Hansen's face contorted; veins stretched in white tracery under the skin of his cheeks. "Listen, why don't you let me alone? Sure, I'll be in good shape. But let me worry about it, see? I'm sick as hell of your fussing and nagging."

"Sorry," Moran said, with a flush. "Nerves, I guess. Didn't

realize how it must seem to you. All right; I'll let you sleep."

The other turned his back again. Hansen stretched himself out on the cool metal of the floor. The cabin was quiet, too quiet; he missed the hum and throb that would have been there if they'd been using the Donlin engines. This etheric drive was ghostly; no sound, no vibration, no crushing sense of acceleration when you were building power.

But he didn't trust it. Too many damned machines nowadays. Machines and more machines all the time. More machines than men pretty soon. Then what? That would be a hell of a fix, if the machines got bright ideas. Thank God, the devils in the dynamos couldn't think. Couldn't they, though? He didn't trust a machine, any kind of machine. Didn't trust them—

A minute later Moran came over and stood looking down at the big blond body stretched on the floor. Hansen slept, restlessly, muttering, voicing stifled groans, rolling a little from side to side.

"A weak sister," Moran said with contempt. "A job like this and they give me a load like him to carry."

He raised his eyes upward, his glance passing through the transparent dome of the control room to touch the steely stars. He saluted them with a lifted fist.

"Hard, aren't you?" He grinned, showing small pointed white teeth. "Hard and secretive and stolid. You don't give yourself away. Me—I'm like you, and I'm glad. To hell with the weak sisters!"

The ship plunked, like a thrown knife, across the empty depths and vacant canyons that gaped between the shaky platforms of the winging worlds. Jupiter loomed close, a haven and a target, but still the Hole stretched like a black wound unfolding in dark flesh. The ship might yet be an unwilling lance forced to probe that wound.

Moran rocked on his two legs, defying and adoring the angry lights that broke the bleakness of those dark skies. Ebony infinity surrounded him, engulfed him, submerged him with a roar of mental surf, yet he remained a rounded entity, complete and unbroken as he had been since he had been cut as a flap from his mother's flesh, since he had emerged as a skein from her skein.

He was a man; he was unique. There were millions very like him, but they were not as he was in all ways. This vision of the void smashed against his eyes, became a part of him, but he was not even now merged with this hungry immensity; like a blind amoeba, the universe extended pseudopodia to take him, to absorb him, but he remained unsoftened and unabsorbed. He was a man; he was unique.

Suddenly he put his head back and laughed, freely and fully, without making any sound.

IV.

Hansen, shivering, suddenly came awake. The shadow of a man's body was over his face; Moran had knelt close to him, was shaking him. He lay still for a minute, frowning, trying to think what it was that seemed so strange. Then he knew; the floor quivered under him in ripples of rhythmic vibration. The Donlin engines were operating. That meant—

Moran, watching him closely, saw realization creep into the half-opened eyes.

Nodding, the captain said somberly: "I thought I'd better waken you. Though there's nothing you can do. Except wait."

Hansen stood up, not straight, because his shoulders slumped and he had the look of an old man again in his face. He groaned. "Why didn't you let me sleep? When I'm awake, I've got to think. I don't want to think."

Moran sneered: "Soft belly! You're afraid?"

"Yes," Hansen said. "Of myself."

He walked slowly over to the chart; when he saw what was mirrored there, he had no need for words. The green sliver of light had left the scarlet arc; slowly the blob of green glow slid toward the edge of the black smear. Hansen coverd his face with his hands.

"No good," Moran said softly. "Dance to the music, friend. The ship's going under."

"How long have you known?" Hansen asked; his voice was tired.

"Just saw it now. Everything seemed to be all right until a minute ago. Then something slipped. I could feel it, as if the ship had lurched on one side. The dials didn't register a thing.

No warning. But when I looked at the chart—I saw what you saw."

Hansen dropped his hands at his sides. "The Hole—how far away do you think it is?"

Moran thought an instant. Then: "About a million miles, I'd say." He was so cool, so calm, so indifferent; he didn't seem to feel anything at all.

Damn him, Hansen thought. But aloud: "Then we've got about an hour."

"That's it." Moran said pleasantly. "If we keep this speed. But we're accelerating, see. The Hole exerts a definite pull; that bears me out. I always thought it was a kind of vortex, which naturally would develop suction."

"Stop!" Hansen screamed. He was pale around the eyes. "I can't stand much of that. Save your damned drivel for a classroom lecture in space school when you're retired—if you think you'll ever see Korna-on-Mars again."

"I'll see it, all right," Moran said quietly. "So will you, if you hang onto your guts. All we've got to do is sit tight, and when the time comes, I'll turn the cube; we'll take our swing along the dimension line, swing back, and the Hole will be behind us, Jupiter dead ahead. Swell!"

Like a madman, Hansen leaped at him. Without preamble, without words, the navigator sprang. Moran, his mouth gaping in a face suddenly left vacant by complete astonishment, fell backward and went down. His head smacked the stellite flooring of the cabin, the angry glow went out behind his eyes, and his body stiffened to a dead weight in Hansen's frenzied grip.

Hansen laughed, looking at the lolling head, the limp body.

"How's that, eh? Swell, huh! How does it feel to be dead, hard guy? How does it feel?"

Moran didn't answer, because he couldn't. Hansen jumped up, moving with a jerky nervous energy, and crossed the cabin to the seal in the wall. He touched a stud, the gimbaled plug dropped out, revealing the ladder seemingly stretching "down" but really going back into the passenger section. He looked over his shoulder; the automatic pilot held the controls, working smoothly and silently.

He scrambled along the ladder, his legs shaking. At the end

of it, a long corridor opened, with numbered cells on either side. He stared at the closed doors blankly; he didn't know what cell she occupied. She hadn't told him, because he hadn't asked her. Before, he hadn't wanted to know; he had been afraid.

Suddenly a door a little distance from him slid into the wall and Tam Graham came into the corridor. She saw him; eyes lighting, she hurried toward him. She was as beautiful as he remembered. For her he had killed; for her he would kill again, if need be.

She came up to him. "Something strange happened," she began breathlessly. "Did you feel it? The ship seemed to go over on one side. There's nothing wrong?"

"Everything's wrong," he said, face grim. "Come with me."

"You're going to take me to the C cabin?"

"Yes."

"But what's wrong? What's happened?"

"I'll tell you when we get forward," he said swiftly. "Are you coming?"

"Of course!"

"Then hurry," he said, his voice strange. "I can't take anybody else, you know. After all, I couldn't save every one of them, could I? Couldn't get twenty-eight people in the C cabin to begin with; silly to think of it. Though there'll be more room when we've thrown Moran out."

He pushed her ahead of him. Going along the ladder, she went first; he followed very closely, his breath puffing. When they were both inside the control room he turned and closed the seal. It seemed to take almost the last of his strength. The blood had been siphoned from his face; he was the color of paper. There was something wrong about his eyes; they didn't seem to focus.

"Here we are," he said. "All nice and cozy. You and I and a dead man."

It was then, looking beyond him, that the girl saw Moran flattened against the floor. Calmly, she stepped a little closer to Hansen and lifted a cool hand gently to his hot face; she covered his eyes an instant.

"Rest a minute," she said soothingly. "You've been going too fast. Close your eyes. Think straight. Something has slipped away behind your eyes, but it will feel its way back, if you go carefully. Don't get excited."

She took her hand away. Hansen had shut his eyes and had been rocking on his heels, listening to the rhythm of her voice. When he opened his eyes, very slowly, the horrible brightness she had seen before was no longer there.

His eyes seemed a little vacant and washed-out; they looked curiously new, as if he was a child, without experience at all, without many memories, without the impressions and sensations that the years and the actualities of living had recorded on his brain. He said, stumbling with his words:

"Something important happened, but I can't remember what it was. Just a little while ago. Maybe if I take a little time to think, it will come back to me."

She walked past him and stopped, near the chart. She had no knowledge of these things, but the record written in light was plain to read—the ship was slipping into the Hole. Now the meaning of Hansen's queer flood of words was clear to her. They were doomed, and Hansen hadn't been able to face the fact. But he had thought of her, and he had come to her with the purpose of somehow protecting her against the death that loomed for them all; he had wanted to save her.

But Moran—his silence, his immobility, the crumpled position of his body, the thin trickle of scarlet flowing from his head—that didn't seem to fit in. She knelt, held the captain's head in her lap, wiped away the blood; there wasn't much blood, but the blue bruise at the back of the skull was very ugly. Still he wasn't dead, or dying, and Hansen had spoken of a dead man.

"Is this the man you meant?" she asked softly, looking across at the navigator.

Hansen still stood like a sleeper in a dream, vacantly staring.

"Is this your dead man?"

Hansen jerked around. "He isn't dead, then?"

"No. Stunned."

Hansen laughed a little, very bitterly. "I might have known. You can't kill the devil."

"You—you tried to kill him?"

"Hell, yes!"

"But why?"

"Why?" Hansen muttered. "I had a damned good reason, beautiful lady; he was willing to let you die. He didn't want to let me save you, and I had to save you."

The girl lifted her head and looked at the navigator soberly. "We're all going to die. I've seen the chart. The ship's driving toward the Hole."

"Yes," Hansen said chuckling, "But we're not all going to die. You and I and Moran—we're safe. We're going to live."

"I'm afraid you're a little mad," Tam said softly. "How can that be?"

"We're in this cabin. As long as we stay here, we're safe. Moran knows. Moran knows how to work the gadget. That thing there, against the wall—he calls it a dimensional converter."

The girl turned her eyes toward the sinister flower; it was beautiful and terrible. Fascinated, she asked:

"How does it work?"

Hansen's face drew together in a sudden tight mask. He said heavily: "I don't know. Moran can explain it to you, maybe. He knows. When the time comes, he'll turn that little cube in the niche in the wall, and this thing will shift the C cabin and everything in it across the dimensional line. That will happen just as the rest of the ship strikes the Hole.

"But we won't be in the ship, understand? This cabin is like a ship inside a ship; we'll be in it, and Moran says it will be in a million other places—I've just happened to think. The cube—you've got to know the angles before you can adjust it; like a safe, you've got to have the combination. And Moran is the only one who knows the combination."

He stared stupidly at the man on the floor. "And I've knocked him out. We've only got a little less than an hour, before the ship hits the Hole. I'm a fool."

The girl lifted her bright head. "Then we've got to do something. I don't believe there's any concussion. He's stunned; that's all. We can try to bring him around."

"Sure," Hansen said eagerly. "Sure, that's it. Maybe we've still got a chance, darling."

"Have you got any cold water?" the girl asked; her face was calm, evidencing no emotion.

Hansen said: "I'll get it—to put on his head. That's the thing they always do, isn't it? Sure, we've got some. We've got water, synthe-food, everything. I told you this was a ship inside a ship."

"All right!" Tam cried. "I'll take your word for it. Now get me the water."

He rubbed one hand across the back of his neck, grinning sheepishly. "Yeah; I'm talking too much, I guess. I feel kind of funny. I can't think straight or something."

He went over to the W-generator, returned with a flask full of cold, absolutely colorless fluid. "Synthetic," he said in queer voice, "but *he* won't know the difference, will he?"

"Give me the flask," Tam said.

He handed it to her like an obedient child, his round eyes adoring her with a vacant intensity. Shivering a little, she commanded:

"Now go sit down somewhere. You're tired; I can see you're very tired, I'll try to bring Moran around. There's nothing for you to do."

Solemn-faced, he saluted her, giving her the full ritual of the space code. "Right, chief!"

He walked to the control board, now ablaze with warning lights futilely signaling that the ship was off course. Buzzers and bells made a subdued clamor at his approach, and as his body came within range of the photo-electric eye, the automatic pilot quietly disconnected itself.

"Damned clever!" he said dizzily, "Damned clever, these machines! Except now they're no good. No good at all. Can't save us, can you? Can't save us, you clever little clicking devils. I better sit down."

He dropped heavily into the pilot's seat and rested his twitching face in his hands. He began to groan softly to himself, muttering over and over: "I'm sick, I'm sick, I'm sick as hell."

It was the wailing of a frightened child.

The girl, leaning close to Moran, rubbed his cold temples with the tips of her fingers. Quiet and steady, her warm hands traveled over his forehead. Then she took the flask of water and let the liquid fall, one icy drop at a time, on the blue swelling at the back of his skull. He shifted his head feebly, whispered:

"Who are you? Thanks, thanks; that feels good. I can't see you yet, but you've got fine hands, soft hands. You're a woman. Get away. No women allowed in this cabin. Get away from me!"

His eyes went wide all at once, blazing like suddenly lighted windows, and his hatred gleamed out at her, mingled with a curious fear. She sensed instantly that he hated her because she was a woman and yet he was afraid, afraid to melt the bars he had welded around him long ago, afraid he might yield to a little tenderness and warm human feeling. He was a scientist first and only human now and then.

"I'm Tam Graham," the girl said simply. "Didn't Hansen mention me?"

He struggled up on his elbow, pulling his head from her lap. He was terribly conscious of the scent of her enveloping him.

"Hansen. I see, I see! He brought you here. He thought he'd killed me, so he was going to put you in my place. You know about the converter?"

"Yes," Tam answered. "I know."

"Then why did you call me back? I was very close to the gate of death. The gate was opening, and suddenly I was pulled away. Something took hold of me and wouldn't let go. That was you."

The girl whispered: "I just couldn't let you die. Unfortunately, I'm a Christian. By your creed of scientific savagery, I'm soft. But I couldn't let you die even though I knew you were my enemy."

Strength was returning to Moran's body in a creeping tide. He had his armor on again, all over; he had no weak spots showing. He grunted, the sound full of contempt.

"You're lying, of course. Probably don't realize it yourself, but you are lying. Overlaid with all that careful rationalization of humanity and Christianity, there's a real reason why you revived me. I'll know as soon as I've talked with Hansen. Hansen can't hide anything from me—that's why he tried to murder my body."

With a grinding effort, he sat up. The room was a broken blur of lights and shadings; he squinted his eyes with a painful concentration and waited, beating down the taut nausea that crept over him. His head ached horribly, but he ignored it.

"Where's Hansen?" he demanded, after an instant.

The girl glanced at him. "Right before you. In the pilot's seat. Can't you see him?"

"Yes; of course," Moran growled. The room began to settle down around him. Pieces fell into place until the shape of the walls, the glow of the lights, the contours of the many mechanisms that crowded the cabin, were no longer a puzzle; things were not quite the same, but he made out a painful semblance of reality.

"Your eyes," the girl said. "They're queer. You're—you're not blind?"

Moran laughed. "You may wish I was before I've finished with you two—but I'm not. I'm in pretty good shape. I can handle you and that murderer. I've just figured out why you brought me around. Hansen remembered that he hasn't got the combination to the cube. He couldn't work my magic. That makes me boss again. He'll do what I say because he has to."

The girl said fiercely: "One thing you'd better consider. He isn't right in his head. If you push him too far he'll go at you again. If you don't want to die—"

"I've been very near to dying," Moran whispered, his eyes receding. "And it isn't bad. It isn't bad at all. In fact, it's quite pleasant. You'll like it."

The girl stood up, tight-lipped. "What do you mean?"

"It's your turn," Moran answered, flat-voiced. "Hansen is going to take you back to the rest of the sentimental cattle who threw their right to live away by coming aboard this ship. You were warned, weren't you? They told you at Korna you could probably expect death."

"I was warned," the girl said, looking down. She stood very still, her breath making a faint rattle in her throat. "Give Hansen the order. If he obeys your command, I'll go."

Moran got on his hands and knees and then pulled himself to his feet with a jerk. He swayed a little, but remained erect; the muscles in his hard hands knotted together and his veins were big with blood, but he stayed on his feet.

He shouted: "Hansen!"

The man in the pilot's seat turned, ceasing his low mumble. Empty eyes regarded iron eyes:

"Yes, commander?"

"Take this girl to the ladder. She goes aft. You know no women are allowed forward here."

The dazed blond giant stumbled to his feet. "Yes, commander."

The girl shut her eyes; with pale lips she whispered to Moran: "This is your victory, scientist. Glory in it!"

Moran braced his legs wide apart. He regarded her without passion, without animus; his hatred, his fear, were both gone, or pushed far under the surface of his thoughts; unguarded by his will, his brain had experienced a rebirth of emotion, but his control had returned. He was dispassionate. He sat in the seat of his consciousness and touched the studs, worked the levers, turned the switches of the efficient mechanism he had made of his body.

"It isn't a question of victory, woman. We decided on a plan for this emergency. His life is more valuable to me than yours; his brain is better than yours. The cells of his cerebral cortex are stored with intricate technical knowledge upon which I may need to draw. You have nothing; you are only a woman. There are many women."

"There are many men."

"You are pleading?"

The girl bowed her bright head. "I find myself—afraid. I'm sorry. Dying may be pleasant, as you say it is, but life to me is more pleasant. I've got so much to live for."

"How very original!" Moran said softly. "You're unselfish. You're a Christian—yet you're pleading for yourself. You're willing to stay here with Hansen and myself, where you have at least a chance for life, rather than go back there with those who have been your companions. Are none of them your friends? Do none of them mean anything to you?"

The girl tightened her hands together. "Yes, yes! But I can live without them. It's not for myself so much that I want to go on living."

"I see," Moran said. "There's a man on Jupiter. You're going to him."

"Yes," the girl whispered. "After ten years."

"Yours is a great love," Moran said soberly. "I'll grant that. But what about all these others on the ship? Do you think they came on this voyage, risking everything, because they were stirred by a small desire or a puny longing, by faint friendship or light love?"

"Ours is a rare thing," the girl said proudly. "An equal love. His is no greater than mine; mine is no greater than his. He loves, and he is loved. I love, and I am loved."

The vacant voice of the blond giant said, all at once: "The woman stays, commander. Here. With us."

Moran hit him with a gouging glance. "You're noble, of a sudden. If she stays, we all three die."

"You mean—" the girl cried.

"Listen," Moran said. "Dimensional mechanics aren't like simple arithmetic. The converter is inconceivably delicate. Hansen—you remember the examination, the physical searching and pounding, to which we submitted before we left Korna-on-Mars?"

"I remember," the giant said, wandering in a maze.

"We were weighed, down to the last molecule. The lines of our bodies were measured with calipers. Our uniforms were fitted and shaped to a certain size. Every mechanism in this room was treated the same way; dimensionally photographed. Those dimensional pictures were fed into the calculators while the converter was being assembled and powered. The converter will swing you and me along the dimensional line, bring us back somewhere inside this cabin, maybe a few inches off center, but we'll make allowances for that. The girl can't go. Nobody else can go. The converter is set to handle two bodies of a certain weight, a certain size, a certain shape. See?"

Hansen turned his pleading, bewildered eyes on the girl. "I tried to save you, didn't I, didn't I? But I guess he's right. He's always right. Now I can't do any more."

The girl raised her hands and touched her hair carelessly. Something like laughter pulsed from her white throat. "You've been grand, space man. You've tried to be a hero, haven't you? All right—I won't let you down."

She looked straight into Moran's hard face. "You've saved me in spite of myself, scientist."

"I don't get that."

"I crawled at your feet, begging for my miserable little life. I thought I was important because I was a woman, because I loved a man, because love is a rare thing in the scheme of the universe. But I see it now—love isn't rare. It's common. There are millions on Earth who have the kind of love I thought I shared with one man alone.

"It's glorious to think of that. I'll think of it when I'm dying—back there with those plain little people you called 'sentimental cattle.' I realize now, I'm not important in myself; only what I had was important. And the universe is overflowing with it. If I didn't believe that, if I thought that kind of tenderness would die with me, I'd fight you. But it won't die. It never dies."

Hansen followed her across the room, opened the seal.

He watched her go along the ladder; for a long time he could see her bright head, held high like a torch; then that, too, vanished in the gloom that crept over the back part of the ship.

"Close that seal and lock it home!" Moran ordered with sudden urgency. "We've only a minute longer."

Hansen turned around; his hands were damp with some kind of moisture that had fallen from his face. He blinked his eyes.

"She was glorious!"

Moran was at the chart, muttering calculations and abstruse formulae.

He called over his shoulder: "Take three steps from the seal and lie down on the floor. Close your eyes. The swing along the dimension line is bound to knock us both cold, and we may as well be comfortable. When I've set the cube to reverse itself, I'll be there beside you."

Hansen took three stiff steps into the room, his knees jerking like those of an automaton. He flattened, folded his arms on his chest, shut his eyes. He whispered, hugging himself: "I'm so tired—"

Moran touched the cube in the wall and sprang back from the blaze of burning brightness that seemed to splash outward from the brilliant surfaces. Blinded and reeling, he felt his way along the floor of the cabin, stumbled into Hansen's body, and sank down, bruising his shoulders on something metallic and admanant.

Sensations left him, and perceptions he had no more. His world of being was not black, but blank.

The control cabin became riotous with ropes of light—light visible and invisible, shaded and colorless, warm as flame and cold as space—

V.

When Moran returned to the controls of the mechanism that was his body, he felt like a stranger in an old house; there were so many things that seemed familiar, yet none of them responded to his presence as they might have to a remembered master. He had been gone so long, he had traveled so far away, that his body had forgotten him.

He struggled to get back into his own brain; to crawl within the shell that had been his; grimly he attached himself to nerve centers and dug into the folded convolutions of his cortex. Then he got home—contact! He sent messages, and faint responses returned from the far-reaching periphery of his nervous system. He gave commands, and there were feeble efforts at obedience.

He was very cold. His body seemed to have taken on a frozen rigidity while he had been absent. Now he could sense the fire of awakened life climbing his body, circling dead nerve ends, spanning some still sleeping synapses, moving forward in little aching pulsations. The hot broth of his blood began to circulate, halting an instant to burn some knotted cold spot from his arteries, then booming and roaring through the great valves around his heart.

His heart woke; there was a heavy blow against his chest, racking him all over with dull pain. Something thudded and thundered against the walls of his body cavity, hurled his blood stream outward in spurting fountains that filled his empty veins; then began a regular thumping and pounding, like the beat of compression engines. His heart had begun to throb.

Still he didn't move, because as yet he could not. Caught somewhere in a dusty corner of his brain was the impulse that could tell his muscles his bidding, but it took him a little time to reach into his mind and remember where the nerve spark lay hidden.

He was sure of one thing only—he was alive. He could move. He heard himself breathing. He felt the pound of his heart beating the reluctant blood through his veins. In a minute he would open his eyes and he would see—What?

For a little while he lay where he was, waiting. He did not know what he expected. There was no change. All was quiet. He stopped his breath an instant—complete silence. He could hear nothing then except the loud sound of his own heart.

There was something smooth and hard-surfaced under his body, holding him up, supporting him. Then he remembered—he must be lying on the floor of the control cabin. Exultation quivered through him; the cube had worked, evidently; they had gone along the dimensional line and returned. Successful experiment! Write that down. Score another victory for science.

He wrenched his eyes open. For an instant he got the full glare of a bright cold light full in the face. Then he was blind again, and the black dark was so deep around him that he seemed more blind than he had been before. But the darkness fell away, a layer at a time, until he could see again.

Very carefully, because he could hear his muscles creak and groan like tight wire, he put his hands behind him, braced himself first on his arms, then pulled himself to one elbow, and at last sat up.

He looked around. The room was familiar to him, almost the same as he remembered it from the time he had glanced at it last, and yet it was not the same at all. It was still the control cabin of the *Star Ship Invincible,* but he was lying on the floor under the pilot's seat; there had been a perceptible shift, then, in his space-time position. Of course! Couldn't expect the thing to work perfectly. He would probably notice other changes.

The lights were turned on, just as they had been at the instant the ship had gone into the Hole; cold Benson globes, all white, snowy glow, harsh and direct, casting thick black shadows in straight lines. He looked at them steadily for a minute, sitting cross-legged like an Oriental and staring upward.

"Queer effect!" he muttered slowly.

A little shiver went over him. After all, this whole room and everything in it had been subjected to an unprecedented change, taken over by an alien force; he couldn't be surprised at anything, if he was going to be logical. But what an opportunity—he had the chance of making a critical study at firsthand of the results of a unique experimental undertaking. He'd have to be impersonal, dispassionate; even if there had been changes in his own body.

"Record everything on a tape spool," he admonished. "Mustn't forget that."

He couldn't get his eyes away from the lights. All the round white globes had a reddish halo, and the light they gave was shot through with black twisting, streamers, impalpable, intangible, like the shadows of shadows.

With difficulty, he took his glance from the Benson globes. He looked at the control set-up. Queer, very queer! The great balanced cylinder of the control base was out of line, slanted wrong; it was the wrong shape. The cylinder seemed to stretch away interminably, gleaming all over with reflected glare that hurt his eyes, as if this brightness was full of little sharp burning spears. The pilot's dais had been touched with the same luminous veneer, gave the same illusion of distortion and distention.

"Elegant!" Moran said. His voice rang hollow, but he wanted to hear himself talk. "Very elegant, indeed—I don't think. I wonder if I'm going to be sick."

He felt that if he sat still any longer he would be. He got on his feet. His legs wavered like rubber stilts under him. Rubbing the back of his hand across his forehead—his hand came away damp—he glanced down at himself; there appeared to be something odd about the shape of his feet, but he couldn't make out exactly what it was.

All at once he was taken about the middle by a hammering nausea; he had hoped to avoid it by standing, no good, evidently. The sensation that shook him was more physical than chemical, he knew that; a mere contraction of his smooth muscles due to shock and nerve tension.

Yet it was odd, very odd. He'd never been sick like this before. An uncontrollable trembling began in his rubbery legs and shot over his body in vicious recurrent waves. The trembling, the vibration in his legs, the torn soreness of his muscles, had no great significance for him then. Later he was to think strange thoughts.

The first step he took, his left knee gave way, as if the bones had melted. He fell, hitting the floor hard. No sensation at all; that was the queerest thing yet. His body must still be numb from its long freezing.

He got up, feeling stronger. He had better luck the second time he tried walking. Looking at the polished floor of the cabin, which was bright as a mirror, he saw that he wobbled like a duck, yet it was locomotion. He wondered, as be began to take a few steps cautiously, why he wasn't hungry. But how long had it been since they had made the dimensional swing? It might have been a millenium; it might have been only a minute ago.

He didn't think he would want food again for a long while. He felt full and warm inside now, and throbbing with a curious pulse of exultation; he had an unreasoning desire to leap up and touch the "ceiling" of the control room. He actually tried it, but fell back after going upward about five feet, which seemed to prove that the ship's gravity grids were in operation. The ship—was he in the *Star Ship Invincible*, or in the control cabin floating free in space? If the cabin had left the ship behind in the Sink Hole, the cabin was now a small ship itself.

He crossed to the visi-plate above the Danler navigation chart. The plate still operated; a faint blue aura surrounded it. He touched a button and the blue became black, the black of outside space. Stars! The plate was speckled all over with perforations of light. In the distance, receding, he saw a web of darkness deeper than infinity; a black hole in the void so dark that it was a purple scar blotting out the stars behind it.

As he stood there, he was conscious of a humming that came through the silence. The automatic switch had jerked along its slot, and the special Donlin engines in the cabin had taken up their beat. He looked down; there was a slight luminescence rising from the gravity grids in the floor plating. Good; the power circuits inside the cabin were unbroken.

There was good air for him to breathe, warm and slightly

scented, as it had been before he had gone down into that sea of blackness. It seemed to be all right again everywhere, except for that curious impression his eyes took in every time he stared at anything for very long. There was a scrambling of his vision, so that he briefly thought he could see the air he was breathing, as a white vapor sucked in and out by his lungs. The great glowing panels of the direction board were twisted out of focus, indefinitely extended behind themselves in blurry reflections, as if they were partly shadows and partly real.

Then he saw Hansen, still crumpled on the floor. He took two quick steps, bent down and touched the other. The navigator's skin was so cold all over that it crackled under the tips of Moran's fingers like frozen fire. Moran turned back the other's eyelids with his thumb and looked at the balls; the man's eyes were turned upward in their sockets and showed all whites.

To any evidence the blond giant was dead. Moran slapped him in the face. He didn't move. Not a muscle jerked or quivered. His jaw didn't even take on any greater color. It remained ice cold and very white—a dazzling ivory pallor. There seemed to be absolutely no blood under the skin of Hansen's cheeks. Moran had seen a man once who had been found frozen in a glacier on Earth, and he had been like that.

Then Moran looked again at Hansen's eyes. The lids had begun to slip shut, as if pulled by springs, but, as Moran watched, Hansen seemed to exert a savage effort, and the eyelids stopped just short of covering the under edge of the eyeballs. Then Moran couldn't believe that Hansen was dead.

Moran bent over him a second time. Very carefully, the scientist took a thumb and held the eyelids back, kept the pressure until when at last he let go, Hansen's eyes remained opened and fixed. Now Moran was sure there was a gleam somewhere in their dazed depths—a spark, grimly struggling upward, attempting to find some way of signaling.

His telepath headgear was still on his body; Moran saw it hanging loose on the belt of his emergency suit. Moran picked up the narrow band of silvery metal and slipped it in a loop around the cold temples. Then he put on his own helmet and concentrated his thoughts in a tight beam of mental energy.

Urgently he prodded the inert brain of the limp giant, then waited. If Hansen was conscious enough to will a single labored thought, contact would be made; Moran's alert intelligence could bring him to awakening.

Taut, Moran crouched, waiting. Hansen's mind was dark, calm as a placid pool, so far as Moran could probe into it without the other's will aiding him.

Moran roared, in a great soundless bellow: "Come out of it, space man! I command you!"

And Hansen moved. The eyes turned. Moran leaned very close, glaring into that frozen face.

"You've heard! Now obey!"

Creaking, the stiff lips parted, a little puff of breath came out, a faint groaning whisper: "Yes, commander."

Moran tore off his headgear triumphantly, sprang up, ran to the W-generator, got water. A cold sparkling rain fell in Hansen's face.

"Enough!" Hansen grunted in a hoarse voice. "What the hell you trying to do—drown me?"

Moran felt better all over. Now he had some one to command, some one to feel superior over, a man to perform obediently at the urge of his will. He warmed; it wasn't good for him to be alone. Even this fool offered a kind of companionship.

"I couldn't drown you," Moran said, grinning. "You've been dead once, to all intents and purposes. You can't die twice—or can you?"

"So the damned thing worked!" Hansen exclaimed with awe. "We've swung along the dimension line, and we've got back, shipshape. That's magic!"

"Magic?" Moran shouted, swelling with anger. "Don't be a superstitious fool. That's science!"

"About the same, isn't it?" Hansen asked.

"No; it isn't," Moran growled. "Don't be an ape."

"Have it your way," Hansen agreed submissively.

Moran stared at him, very sober. For some reason the blond man seemed smaller than he had been, his face was wrinkled and wizened into a dried mask, and his legs were twisted to a queer shape. Moran wondered if he would be able to walk, using those dead legs.

Yet when Moran stared into those strange eyes at close range, he saw a reflection of himself, and *he* seemed to be the same as the navigator was—turned and shifted in his body, as if the center of his equilibrium had been reversed. Moran thought, so there have been great changes in us, as in the machines crowding this room. But—how deep did the alterations go? His calm curiosity probed for the answer to that question.

Hansen observed, in a hoarse voice: "Say, you look damned funny! Like you've had the bends, or something. Been space sick?"

"Listen," Moran said harshly. "You don't think we took that joy ride in the grip of dimensional forces and got away clean, do you? Sure, I look funny. So do you. It's one of the—the changes. You'll notice other things that are—damned funny."

"Maybe I talked too fast," Hansen mumbled. "Maybe the converter didn't work after all. Where are we? Where's the Hole?"

"Behind us," Moran stated, calm-voiced. "We're on course, and close to Jupiter. Take a look in the v-plate."

Hansen got up and went over to the little screen. The Sink Hole didn't show there at all now, nor any trace of it. The sky looked calm, and it was black the way it always had been since Hansen had been aspace, but it was the kind of black a man can look at and understand; there were stars in it, different colors, and the Sun away off in the distance like a red-hot blinking eye put there to watch over you. Jupiter the giant seemed closer, and Hansen thought with sudden hope that they now had at least an even chance of making the Dome.

Moran crossed the cabin and examined the three cylinders standing against the curved wall. That wall was blank, had no glassite porthole, and most of it was covered with a curled mesh of wire, an intricate network of apparatus, because the three tanks carried all the little ship's supplies of air and water and synthefood. If something went wrong in any part of that maze—

Hansen watched him as he tested the tanks. He came around on his heel, face impassive.

Hansen said: "Well?"

"Enough there, if we're careful."

Hansen expelled his breath gratefully. "We're in luck."

"Luck? No. It was calculated how much supplies we'd need before the ship left Korna. The calculations are a little in error, but very little. And I counted on a marginal deviation."

Hansen said: "Oh, hell!"

Then for an instant the navigator felt that something had gone wrong in his eyes. Yet it wasn't that. The truth was that Moran was getting smaller.

"Chief!" Hansen whispered hesitantly.

Moran looked up, eyes tight with an inward struggle. "What?"

Hansen stuttered: "I dunno how to say it. But you—you're kind of shrinking."

"Yes; I know."

Moran kept his cold composure. But his body was terribly changed; he was altogether different from the commander who had shipped with Hansen on the *Invincible*. Then he had been a fairly big man, almost as big as the navigator, and strong as stellite; still young, still with the full look of youth and strength in his face. This was a shrunken little old man.

He came close, stood a moment with his face up against Hansen's. He put out a hand to touch the navigator, and the other jerked back, because that outstretched hand looked like a brown and withered claw. He seemed—he seemed to have caved in upon himself.

Hansen shook; his teeth clicked. "What—what's happening to you, commander?"

Moran grinned crookedly. "You'll know soon, I hope. You've been subjected to the same forces. The effects should be very much the same on you."

"How—how does it feel?" Hansen whispered. "What's it like?"

"Wait," Moran answered confidently. "Just wait. You'll get a dose of this medicine soon enough, friend."

His face was chopped in little wrinkled squares by short bitter lines of agony.

"I'll tell you this much," Moran said with a livid smile. "It isn't very pleasant. Not at all."

"Damn you!" Hansen groaned. "You needn't torture me before my time comes. Why are you always throwing little knives into me?"

Moran didn't answer. He was too intent on keeping any sound of pain from escaping through his lips.

VI.

Moran tightened his mouth; as he did so, Hansen could see a plainly visible sifting and sinking that seemed to go on simultaneously all through his body, as if the orbits of the atoms that composed his flesh had abruptly been decreased in the diameter of their paths and closed in upon themselves.

"I'm still getting smaller?" Moran said after a few seconds.

Hansen nodded. "Every minute I'm standing here I can see it happening. You don't come quite up to my shoulder now, commander."

He seemed to stand there considering something abstract, looking very quiet and detached. He appeared to have gone away off and was observing himself as from a reasonable distance. Before then Hansen had hated Moran very heartily, with the deep hatred of an inferior for a superior mind, but something like admiration crept into the navigator now; the commander was so cool and calm, as if he had climbed out of the shell of himself, somehow, and could stand to one side, regarding himself with no prejudice.

"It'll stop soon, I think," Moran said suddenly. "I've had it once before, right after I woke. Then I didn't realize what was happening to me. I just thought I was getting pretty sick. But now it's plain. All clear."

"You're right," Hansen said, "about one thing at least. It seems to be stopping."

In another instant Moran ceased to shrink. The effects remained; his skin hung in loops and folds all over him, and his cold eyes looked too big for his unraveled face. With difficulty he moved, climbed up on the pilot's seat, and sat with his little legs hanging over the edge of the metal-fabric chair.

Hansen couldn't look directly at him. The navigator said: "Well, what's next? What'll happen after this?"

Moran gave a slow shrug. It was queer to see his skin quiver in a ripple along his loose-jointed shoulders.

"That," Moran said, "is what I don't know—yet."

Hansen didn't move. There was silence between them.

Then Moran said: "I know what it's doing to me, and that it will come to you in a little while, but I haven't quite figured out certain things. I haven't found out why it stops once it gets started, and where it will end if it keeps on. Theoretically, I don't suppose there's any limit at all."

Hansen frowned. "You haven't explained a damned thing to me yet."

"Well, the conditions are paradoxical," Moran said thoughtfully. "There's room in this for some beautiful paradoxes. It's plain that the effects you and I have undergone, along with everything else in this room, are due to the distortion caused by dimensional change. We weren't built to be in a million places at once, see. That's why we can't hold our old shapes; you know, I'm not sure that I'm actually getting any smaller. It's a change in shape, visible to you and me as a change in size."

"Go slow," Hansen said, heavy-voiced. "I'm stumbling along behind you."

Moran grinned. "Our constituent atoms, friend, have been twisted and shuffled around, and they're having a devil of a time finding their places. They've had the most awful wrench they could have got anywhere in the universe; they've been jammed all together, and then stretched structurally outward, and then set free in their old orbits again. But they're not staying put; that's all. They haven't got to a condition of equilibrium yet. That nice balance between attraction and repulsion, between protons and electrons in the nucleus, and electrons outside the nucleus—that balance is overthrown, releasing chaotic forces within the atoms, and naturally the atoms shape the molecules. See?"

"I think so," Hansen muttered. He rubbed a hand across his eyes. "If you're right, and you're always right, time's called for you and me. There's no limit. There's no telling where this thing will stop?"

Moran shook his head. "No. Only there's no guarantee that we'll die, now or later. There was some fault and molecular slippage when I contracted this time. I got out of proportion at least to my eyes and your eyes. That's the reason my skin's loose and I look so queer. If it comes again it may take up the slack. I don't know."

Hansen blinked. "If it stops, maybe we'll be kinds of dwarfs, or something."

"Yes," Moran said. "But I don't think it's going to stop at any imaginable point."

Moran's eyes gleamed; he was fascinated by that thought. He might sink down slowly into a submicroscopic universe. Or if the change was, as he believed, a relative alteration in shape, he might enter a cosmos of different dimensions, a brand-new world, unexplored, opening to his avid gaze, his insatiate curiosity. The possibilities were illimitable for experimental operations. The chance was his.

Then Hansen remembered something. "The ship!" The navigator's voice was hoarse with excitement.

Moran said: "What about the ship?"

"If we keep on getting smaller, and the ship doesn't shrink—how will we eat? What the hell will we drink?"

Moran laughed. "Don't worry about that. Are you hungry now? Fill your belly up then. If you have time to digest it before your contraction begins, you'll be all right."

"Look," Hansen muttered. "If we're eventually no bigger than a drop of water, we're not going to be able to swallow anything of that size. And food—the atoms will be so big they won't go down our throats. Maybe they'll be bigger than we are."

"I've failed to make it clear to you," Moran said. "That's because it's a paradox. We aren't shrinking; we're changing size. The ship isn't shrinking, because it's made of metal; metal's rigid, the atoms are bound tight together. When we came back from the dimensional swing, the metallic molecules fitted together and they've stayed together; but they're not the same. They've changed shape. So have we, only in a different degree."

Hansen didn't say anything, because he couldn't speak. He had begun to diminish in size; at least to Moran's eyes it seemed that he shrank, though Moran's brain accepted it as a relative alteration in shape. An indistinctness seemed to hang about the blond man, like half a shadow. Even the features of his face, which were close to Moran, so close that the commander might have reached and touched them, were vague and blurred.

The contraction ended. Hansen didn't seem mutilated. His body was more in proportion than it had been; his face was tiny, rather wrinkled but perfectly formed; his legs had lost most of their crookedness; his head was set firmly on his neck, his arms and shoulders flowed together in a smooth line.

Hansen whispered: "I can't take much of that."

Sweat dribbled from the end of his chin. His eyes swiveled wildly. He said, in a high-pitched voice:

"We thought we were pretty damned smart, didn't we? Nothing was going to happen to us. We were safe. To hell with the Hole, to hell with those twenty-eight people we murdered! We'd get through, because we had that damned thing you called a dimensional converter. It's got us—it's got both of us around the throat."

He sucked in his breath. "Listen, I'm going to finish this. Maybe this damned shrinking will go on even when we're both dead, but we won't know it. We won't know it, see?"

Moran slid one hand down his side to the metal-linked belt at his hips and touched the round butt of his ionic projector.

He said: "All right. You've got your I-gun. Pull it out, and we'll fire together. That will end it for both of us."

"Sure!" Hansen said softly.

Moran could see the gleaming in Hansen's belt where his hand projector was, and in his brain the commander had a vision of a bright silver thread, hot and white, spiraling across the narrow space between them, striking death home to them both.

Hansen dropped his fingers to the grip of his little gun, but he had no chance to lift it from where it swung at his waist. Moran had drawn, thumbed a stud, sent an arrow of flame scorching into the blond man's face.

Hansen swayed backward, bending at the knees; he went over, hitting on his shoulders and head. There was a slight thump, like knuckles striking metal; that was the sole sound, except for the snake-like hissing of Moran's flame-thrower.

Moran tossed the little gun away. "I'm ready," he said softly, looking at the stars. "I'm not going to die."

VII.

For three days there had been rain on Jupiter the giant. The rain was scalding hot; it turned to steam as it fell, burned the ground where it struck. The great bronze Dome of the interplanetary station felt the touch of that liquid fire; scales were melted off the outer shell of the Dome, metal ran down in molten waves.

The air above and around the Dome was crowded with tortured flying things, the bizarre creatures that inhabited the upper levels of the great planet. There were strange currents going upward through the atmosphere; the laws that governed the magnetic forces of worlds were seemingly broken.

Over the Red Spot was created a reverse field of gravity. They observed it from the Dome; flying things passing that way were hurled outward at savage speed into the far reaches of the atmosphere. The Red Spot itself remained as always—an enigmatic sea of luminescent flame.

First into the writhing atmosphere above the Red Spot the little ship from space had entered. There was no down pull of Jupiter's immense gravity to increase its terrific speed, but instead was this magnetic repulsion that checked the ship's free fall, wrenched it partly off its course. The controls of the small ship were locked; it traveled along the Walton Arc that had its ending within the interplanetary station.

The little ship fell in a slow bright curve through Jupiter's thick and steamy atmosphere, crumpled its silver shell into the red ground two miles from the Dome.

The electro-telescopes in the station had followed the strange ship in from space. A man came up into the little room at the top of the Dome where John Graham, G-16, sat silently at his key. The man saluted and said in a stiff voice:

"The ship Garth told you a day ago we were to watch for—"

"Yes," Graham said, grim-faced. "I saw it fall."

"You're to take charge of the search party, G-16. The station commander's orders."

Graham nodded. "I obey," he said gently. "I always obey orders."

A day later the rain stopped. Six men ventured out from the Dome, wearing space suits, breathing Earth's atmosphere. John Graham led them. They had taken readings from direction-finders before leaving the station, and they knew about where the ship had fallen. The search was not long.

The little ship was found, almost undamaged, the curious dull metal of which it was fashioned being neither twisted nor broken; where it had given way it had been forcibly torn apart. It was a strange shape for a space ship. It was like a flying cube, oddly distorted along its angles.

There was a seal in one side of the cube. They broke the seal and Graham went in first. He went in, stumbling.

There was nobody alive inside.

One glance told him that.

For a minute he halted there with the blind agony of his unreasoning disappointment mirrored in his eyes; long ago he had believed he had given up hope, yet evidently there had been a spark still left. He shook himself, swinging his hands, and moved forward into the ship.

It wasn't a ship at all. It was the control cabin of the *Star Ship Invincible.* There was a dead man lying on the floor, the body curiously shrunken.

"Hansen," Graham muttered softly. "Moran?"

No sign of the commander. But in one of the curved seats near the control board he found a spool of metallic tape, and beside it a flash tube for recording messages.

The men from the station had come in quietly behind him and stood staring. One of them asked: "What's that, sir?"

Graham turned and pushed past them, unseeing. He flung back over his shoulder a mutter of words. The man who had spoken glanced around the room.

"He's found some kind of a record. He's going back to the station. We're to stay here with the ship until he gets further orders."

Graham traveled fast to the recording room in the Dome. He sat down, put his eyes to the eyepieces provided, fitted earphones to his head. Then with slow careful hands loosened the clip that held one end of the tape from unraveling; he fed the thin metallic strip into the slot of the translator, touched a dial.

A long time later he reached up slowly and thumbed a stud.

The narrow tongue of metal ceased to flow into the translator. He took off the headphones he had been wearing, tore away the eyepieces. He put his head in his hands and groaned.

Two men had come into the dim room. One was the station commander.

The commander said: "What have you found?"

Graham grinned queerly. "This is the recording made by Captain Moran. It's all there—what happened to the *Invincible*. But it's not a very pretty story."

"I see," the commander said. "What have you done about the little ship we saw fall?"

"I'm having it brought into the Dome. Are there any orders you want to give me?"

The commander hesitated. "No; I don't think so. Wait! We've got to make some disposition of the bodies."

"Bodies?"

"The bodies of Hansen and Moran," the commander said impatiently. "Didn't you find them in the ship?"

"There was only one body," Graham answered, grim-faced. "Moran is still alive—somewhere. He's gone into a different dimensional universe, but he's alive. He recorded everything that happened until his change in size took him beyond body contact with the tape he was using. He even recorded his murder of Hansen."

"He murdered Hansen?" the commander whispered.

"Hansen and my wife," Graham said, very low. "I'm waiting for further orders, sir."

"No orders," the commander said heavily.

Graham traveled upward to the signal room high on the curve of the Dome. His relief stared.

"You're early, G-16. You've an hour yet."

"Let me take over," Graham said. "Let me take over, will you?"

The other shrugged. "All right with me. You're a fool for work. Why don't you get a little sleep?"

"I don't need much sleep these days," Graham said.

He sat down, closed in once more by sky and stars; he looked at the black, pitiless void that was all around him, and the taste of bitterness was in his mouth.

The Radium World

Have you ever listened to the whispers that come out of Mars' Red Deserts? The zina is the most beautiful and deadly of all Mars' deadly and beautiful things.

CAPTAIN GRANT, commanding officer of the Terrestrial space-liner *Trident*, took an unsteady eye from the luminous glow of the Danler spacial navigation chart, pushed back from the curved steel shield of the giant ship's control board, and got up with resolution. There was room for him to stand erect in the tight-squeezed machine maze of the pilot's cabin, but no more. A sudden rebellion rose within him against the hot closeness of the control-room.

He turned a restless eye, normally a steel shade of clear grey, (but at the moment red and jaundiced-looking from over-indulgence in ancient synthecholic) and stared at the stiff straight back of Jimmy Brame, the ship's second officer. The latter's attention was riveted on the graph of a fluctuating pressure-gauge.

"Look here, Jimmy," Grant said suddenly. "You can handle her as well as I can. I do wish you'd go ahead and do it. I'm rather fed up. . . . Damn!" He rubbed an aching head tenderly. "Damn all farewell parties! Suppose I really shouldn't have taken that last one, though. 'At stuff of Tilton's was strong enough to walk. Damn!" He took in the stiff angle of the second officer's Boston back, indicating Brame's private opinion of farewell parties, and those who went in for them, and grinned appreciatively. "Well, I'm shoving off, Jimmy. G'night."

Brame gave him an absent nod.

"Um—deviation point three four two compressor seven check—O.K., sir. G'night."

He did not look up from his graphs. The captain, yawning prodigiously, swung down the companion ladder dropping into the ship's midsection from the bridge. At the bottom he removed carefully from a mysterious pocket of his gold-and-white Fleet uniform the blackened remnant of his old pipe. Use of tobacco is forbidden by the Vice Laws of 2026, along with a great many other things, but Grant had been initiated into the seductive mysteries of the fragrant weed at Harvard-Of-Earth in undergrad days, and had stuck most stubbornly to it since.

If the Vice Board had a man aboard the ship, which was more than likely, the chances were that he'd part with a sizable slice of petty blackmail. (All Vice Agents blackmail as a matter of course.)

Still, he could afford the luxury. The compensation of a commercial space captain these days is most certainly not a pittance, and the giant *Trident* was Star Lines' pet Mars liner.... Besides being the crack ship of the far-flung Star Fleet.

There wasn't a man in the organization who wouldn't have given his eye-tooth for Bob Grant's job. Grant knew it. And he'd bullied Vice men before, the rats!

Defiantly he lit up. The ship's decks were close to desertion—it was nearing midnight (ship chronometer time, of course) and habit had sent most of the crowd of passengers to their sleeping-cabins—so he was reasonably safe from the keen eye of a Vice man. He inhaled deeply, held the pungent bootleg fragrance deep in his lungs until they swelled almost to bursting, and expelled smoke with caution. (Cautiously, because Vice agents have a most annoying habit of materializing out of empty air.)

He took a slow way in the general direction of the sleeping-cabins. At the juncture of two silent deserted corridors he was faced with the necessity of deciding whether to take the direct route to his bunk, or the longer (and safer) circle through O-Deck. He decided upon the observation-deck. After all, the night was still young.

He stood several minutes by the giant glassite look-out

ports of O-Deck. He liked the view from this angle of the ship. It *was* rather immense.

The stars burned coldly in a dark back-drop of absolute black that was tinged very faintly with the soft rose radiation of the Earth-Mars Insulation Beam; Earth was a round blue-green ball in the infinite distances behind; Mars a study in scarlet swimming in the vast space ahead.... He always wondered what might happen if that impervious Beam-Tunnel were to falter for an instant—and let the ship go driving blindly unprotected into the living maelstrom of free space. Of course it couldn't possibly. But he liked to think about it, with the faintest tinge of vicarious horror.

O-Deck at midnight seemed subtly altered from the tense reality of ship "day," changed by some witches' alchemy into a soft vagueness of lights and shadows. An eldritch mingling of starlight slanted down upon the scrubbed clean whiteness of the floor; gilded silver the empty rows of deck-chairs and deserted card-tables; melted the harsh modernistic outlines of the stellite wall paneling into a bizarre white beauty. Grant liked it.

Someone was walking slowly along the corridor. The light footfalls moved softly in the direction of the observation-deck, faded an uncertain instant, and began again from across the floor. Grant's hand jerked guiltily at the forbidden pipe, hesitated, and replaced it in the corner of his mouth. His jaw set. If it were a Vice spy—but of course it wouldn't be. More likely another night stroller, sleepless, restive as himself.

The footsteps quickened abruptly, melted into a queer, half-running, half-stumbling sound, and suddenly stopped dead. A man's voice cursed, the words sliding off into a strange scream. A table toppled over with a muffled crash, closely followed by the tinkle of breaking glass. A chair thudded against the deck-wall, and smashed.

Grant whirled, tensed. His eyes probed the vague blackness of the darkened deck. Shadow-shapes flurried in a corner, and a hurtling body suddenly erupted from them, crashed against the crumpled table, struck the chair, and slammed to the floor.

Grant strained his eyes. The body was that of a man. A man who writhed desperately in a stellite deck-corner, and struck out with helpless fists against his antagonist. Weird antagonist!

Have you ever listened to the whispers that come out of Mars' Red Deserts? Horror tales of the beauty and the silent deadliness of the creatures of those deserts? The zina is the most beautiful, and the most deadly of all Mars' deadly, beautiful things. It is a carnivore, cruel, blood-lustful, horribly cunning. It has the body and head of a flying thing, and the scintillating antennae, the faceted metal eyes of the insect. The eyes are red spots of evil wisdom, like those of some Earth vampire.

Grant caught the glimmer of scarlet eyes, and knew that the man on the floor was battling silently with a zina-vampire. The man's fight was horribly hopeless. No unarmed man can long evade the lightning thrusts of the great hooked beak, withstand the tireless flailings of the giant wings, struggle against the absolute blood-lust of the creature. This man was unarmed. If he had been armed at the beginning, the rush of the zina must have taken him unaware, before he had even time to reach for his weapons.

Grant plunged grimly—and hopelessly—across the shadowed deck, jerking at his Bressler electron pistol as he came. The Bressler is a deadly little thing, capable of belching a hot tongue of burning, flashing death. If he could get in a single shot—

The vampire whirled, in a motion so rapid that his eyes were unable to follow it, and launched its brilliant body savagely upon him. Desperately, he dodged. The needle-beak slid rustling along his shoulder, ripping ruthlessly through the metallized cloth of his uniform, searching out his throat. A long shallow gash opened in the base of his neck.

Stinging nausea filled him. Frenziedly, he struck out with his fists, beat hard against the whirling net of brilliant wings that encircled him. It was the pipe that was really his salvation. Clenched unnoticed in his hand, it landed simultaneously with his knuckles full upon the fleshy underside of the cruel hooked jaw.

Sparks flew wildly, scattering a shower of hot burning tobacco over the gauzy beating wings. A network of flame caught in the glinting silky net, licked hungrily. An agonized thrumming pounded the air, engulfed Grant in a hurricane of blows that knocked him flat on the deck and drove the wind out of his body.

The Thing, forgetful of him, hurled itself backward frantically, beat the great wings against the loathsome body in an effort to extinguish the spreading trickle of tobacco flame.

Grant winced. Something quivered through his prostrate body like a cold shock. The vampire, gradually beating out the fire creeping along its wings, stiffened, staggered erect, and stood motionless, its grotesque bright head tensed on the side, almost as though it were listening. Grant felt the cold shock again, a queer sensation oddly like a mental command. The vampire lifted its scintillating wings and flashed across the dark deck toward the black opening of the center corridor, hung an instant against the jet background, and vanished from sight.

Something spat viciously. Grant, who had half-straightened, flung himself prostrate again, and listened with an icy trickle on his spine to the spiteful crackle of an ion flash that seared the air close above him, leaving in its wake a strong smell of burning ozone. Barricaded behind the bulwark of the overturned card-table, he swept the black corridor opening with a searching flash from his Bressler. Nothing moved, or shuddered to the hot touch of his silver flame-lance.

But when he had finished, convinced that whatever might have shot at him from the corridor had retreated beyond range, he caught the sound of light footsteps receding down the corridor, floating faintly back to him with the echoes of mocking laughter.

The captain got cautiously to his feet and flung the unconscious body of the man he had saved across his shoulder. Keeping the Bressler in evidence in his right hand, he moved carefully up the dim-lighted ramp that connected the observation-deck with the sleeping-cabins above. He did not breathe easily until he was safely in his own room, the door locked, and his man made comfortable in the cabin's lower bunk.

By some miracle the unknown man had escaped serious wound, though his black cloak was torn and ripped savagely at the throat, and he bore several ugly gashes in the bronzed muscle of his neck. The captain got water from the washstand at the head of the bunk and bathed the brown forehead.

The man had a long, melancholy face and jaw, straight fine features, a good nose, and a firm well-made mouth. His chin was like hard-cut granite. His eyes were webbed with a myriad small puckered wrinkles that spoke of long hard hours in the sun. Grant liked what he saw, but was troubled with a conviction that he had once known someone greatly resembling this man.

The man opened his eyes. Grant narrowly escaped a murderous uppercut that began from nowhere and flashed upward in an arc from the bunk toward the point of his jaw. As it was, he took the blow on the shoulder and sat down abruptly.

"Well, of all the—"

The man in the bunk was sitting up. His eyes, which had been hard bits of flint an instant gone, changed subtly at sight of the tattered gold bars clinging to Grant's uniform.

"Your pardon, Captain," he said contritely, helping the indignant Grant to a chair, "I'm afraid I took up where we broke off—out there." He waved an arm significantly toward the cabin door.

"I suppose I have you to thank for the sudden change in the—er—situation. I must say you were Johnny-on-the-spot, Captain. That devil caught me rather on the blind side. I—"

Grant was staring curiously at him. A sudden suspicion grew in the space captain's eyes, broke into dawning comprehension.

"Well, I'll be—Gray!"

"Grant!"

They shook hands warmly, and pounded each other with affectionate blows. Grant had been captain of the now famous 2024 grid squad at Harvard-Of-Earth. Gray, his inseparable roommate and chum, had been one of the most sensational quarterbacks the college's long history had known.

"Whew!" the captain said. "To think how near Harvard's never-to-be-forgotten Gray Ghost came to being zina meat! Jove, Gray, I believe if I'd known it was you I'd have been so paralyzed—"

Gray punched him in the shoulder.

"If you'd known who it was, you wouldn't have gone into that famous line rush of yours, eh? Thank you, Mr. Grant!"

But the captain looked grave.

"What devilment are you up to now, Gray?"

Gray looked so mockly indignant that the captain was hard put to keep from laughter. But he cut off the flow of humorous protests with a knowing hand.

"Listen: somebody aboard ship's after your well-known scalp; and there must be a damned good reason. The murderer's not doing it for pastime, you know!"

Gray nodded soberly.

"I know. I suppose I really ought to tell you after.... There *is* a reason for what happened out there, Grant. A damned good reason, as you say. I think you'd probably die of curiosity if I didn't, so I might as well tell you. Of course, you'll keep it under your hat."

The captain's eyes showed his itching curiosity. He stretched himself out comfortably in a long chair, set his pipe going, and waved an impatient hand.

"This place's double sound-proofed, if you're afraid of spying, Gray. Of course, if you think I—"

Gray looked reproachful.

"I was just wondering how to begin. There are so many places.... But I suppose you might say the thing had its start with Mej-Tel's madness, so I'll begin there." And the following was his story.

CHAPTER II
Space Madness!

I CAME reluctantly out of a thick sleep of utter exhaustion to the somber reality of my sleeping-cabin. The room was dark and very quiet. The faintly luminous face of the clock in the opposite wall pointed at half-a-minute past twelve, ship chronometer time. The warm blackness between my bunk and the clock was perfectly still. And then I heard it again.

A muffled beating sound of someone's fists pounding against the stellite of the cabin-door. A queer choking sound of rapid breathing that I didn't like. It was oddly like the dry rattle of wind in the throat of a dying man. It made me uneasy.

I got quietly out of the bunk and hurried into my clothes. In the space of ten heart-beats I had dressed, crossed the floor in silence, and thrown open the door. I thought I was prepared for whatever might come. But I was not.

It was Jad, my Venusian mate and a man who had been with me several voyages, who stood swaying gently in the opening, his great eyes rolling in a tight face-mask the color of chalk. I will not forget easily the look in those twitching eyes. Utter horror, revulsion, nauseated loathing, all were mixed indescribably in their deep pools. Every muscle in his clean-cut face was taut. Red flecks had gathered at the thin line of his lips. His hand was tight against his throat.

He staggered, and I caught him. His hand came away from his thin throat, and in the dim half-light of the corridor I caught a nauseating glimpse of a ragged knife slash cut deep into the thick muscles at the base of his neck. A sickening torrent of blood spouted from the wound, spread down his blouse to the floor. There was a growing crimson stain on my shirt.

I carried Jad into my cabin and laid him carefully on the single bunk. He made no outcry, though the pain of movement must have been terrific, said nothing except a struggling whisper:

"Mej-Tel—did this. He's gone . . . amuck. Got me. Throat. I'm through, Captain. . . . "

And after that, silence. Silence broken only by the sibilant whistling of his hard-drawn breath, the faint panting of his livid lips; silence that lasted while he watched me apply a crude bandage of surgeon's gauze to the ragged wound. And suddenly the whistling faded to a choking murmur, bubbled faintly, vanished. The breathing from the bunk stopped. I stood a little dazed, bewildered, surging with anger against the murderer.

And as I listened in the hot silence, a crashing sound came from beneath, a faint echo of raised voices mingled in tumult. I drew a sheet over the man on the bunk. Then, unlocking a drawer in the steel desk bolted against the wall, I withdrew my Bressler, which, though seldom enough used, was always charged and kept in good working order for an emergency.

This was an emergency.

The sounds below suddenly increased. I recognized them as coming from the engine-room. Heavy feet thudded on the stairway spiral.

I crouched grimly at the side of the black well dropping from the control-room into the dark depths of the ship's vitals, the Bressler tightened comfortingly in my fist.

A head appeared suddenly in the blackness below me. A taut, twitching, madman's head, with the grinning face-mask of an apparition, a lather of foam tight upon its thick red lips and yellow pointed cannibal teeth, a glowing fire wild-lambent in the single great eye rolling insanely in the leathery dark forehead.

A knife glimmered in the mingled light of the control-room, brandished in the muscular fingers of a giant black fist. A wild cry smashed the hot silence to protesting shreds.

I reached over the stair-rail and drove the butt of the Bressler into the dark face below. The giant only reeled back a little, shook his savage head dazedly at a blow which would have crushed an Earthman's skull to fragments.

Then the knife slashed out and downward, digging a vicious red furrow in the muscles of my protecting, upflung arm. A white hot iron seared my left shoulder.

Frenzied by the pain, I aimed the Bressler blindly at the rolling eye of the madman and released the charge. The bright silver flame tongue licked eagerly at the black face.

I hope never to see that again. Sickened, I turned my head away. Something struck dully on the steps of the stairway, and catapulted down. There was a succession of falling sounds, ending in a sodden impact of flesh on steel—and after that, a heavy silence.

I tore my shirt in strips with my teeth, and fashioned a makeshift sling for my ripped arm. Then, forcing myself, I took torch in hand and descended the steps to the engine-room.

The place was plunged in fetid darkness. In his frenzy, the cook must have encountered the wiring of the night Tomlinson "cold" lamps, slashed out blindly with his knife, and severed the connections. I swung the torch beam in a wide circle.

The white cone of light fell upon a macabre little group of bodies. I saw Gobrentz, the German, lying crookedly against the metal side of the wall, his soft blue eyes gazing peacefully at nothingness. A sudden sickness gripped me when I realized that his head was hanging from his neck by a single thread of tough sinew. Beside the German lay Exham, a little Anglo-Saxon with English written in every thin tight line of him. There was a clean slash in the wiry muscles of the Cockney's stringy neck.

Mej-Tel lay motionless at the foot of the stair, knife still gripped convulsively in his hand. Counting the black devil himself, I had lost four men to madness: Jad, the mate; Gobrentz, a forward ray-man; Exham, a beam operator, and the cook, Mej-Tel. Then—with six men left behind in that miserable little port of Jupiter, four others taken by the intangible plague of space sickness, four slaughtered by this accursed madman, I had left, besides Haj, my engineer, a half-dozen able spacemen with which to navigate the crippled *Sprite*. And twenty was her normal muster!

I cursed the black cook with all the fluency of four years' wandering in the odd corners of the universe. But suddenly I stopped, curses and breath alike strangling with a sense of utter disaster in my throat, when my roving gaze encountered the Tolstoi water generator. It was a smashed ruin! A tangled mass of splashed wiring, broken tubes, battered condensers, testified grimly to the efficiency of the knife of madness.

Rotten, devil's luck! Left here in mid-space with the single bottle of water in my cabin to last the eight of us until we struck Mars! One lone bottle of water to last three days! I stood staring at that broken thing like a man dazed, quite unable to believe the stunning evidence of my senses.

I was aroused by the stirring of the remnant of the crew, which had fled precipitately to the safety of hiding at the first signs of Mej-Tel's madness.

Silent, they gathered quietly beside me, staring hard at the ruins of the Tolstoi apparatus. They knew well enough what it meant—thirst. They were men who had known the tortures of a parched throat before, thirst on the scorching arid plains of Mars' great deserts, in the bleak barrens of the Devil Mountains of Neptune, in a hundred tight corners of the odd places of the Universe. Yet they did not flinch.

Haj, the engineer, shot me a queer glance from his squinting lidless eyes. I looked at him. He was an old Venusian, squat, moist-skinned, gray-faced, possessed of the colorless features of his ancient race. Superstition was deeply ingrained in him. He mumbled tonelessly, eyes now upon the stellite of the floor:

"No water! Surely, there is a curse upon us, Pale One. We have terribly angered Ahj-Teh, God of Wanderers and of Water. His curse is terrible. We—"

I struck him sharply across the cheek with the flat of my hand. I knew that the men were watching with narrowed eyes.

"Shut up, old fool. We *have* water. Water enough, if we waste none, to last us until we strike the Black Well at Deimos. No more of that sort of talk!"

I knew that I was giving them a barefaced lie; and they knew it certainly as well as I did, but with the eagerness of the utterly lost they snatched at the straw. I saw relief in suddenly relaxed faces. Old Haj stared at me for a moment like one dazed, then abruptly recognition, sanity, a great gratitude flooded his liquid eyes.

I flashed my torch on the torn night-wiring.

"Haj! Get to work on this. We've got to have light, you know. And when you've finished, inspect all engines to see what damage, if any, was done them by the madman."

I turned on the spacemen, who still stood staring at the smashed ruins of the Tolstoi. I flung at them:

"Don't stand there like mummies! Welch! Glannel! Turney! You're detailed to clean up this place. It looks like a slaughter house. Filthy. Get to work! Eject those bodies through the aft beam tubes; and take Jad's out of my cabin. Poor devil!"

"The rest of you are dismissed. Get back to your bunks and sleep. Sleep, I tell you! Forget this! Don't think about it, and you'll be all right. And Barham! Stop staring at that Tolstoi! You look a ghost, man. Come out of it!"

I drove them, hurling orders. Haj got hold of the break in the Tomlinson "cold" wiring, and the night lamps gleamed frigidly in a space of minutes. When I had finished with the men, and turned to go up the stairway to the control-cabin, Haj was close following. He reported no visible damage to any of the engines....

Above, in the control room, the two of us studied the navigation chart; a moving red dot on the luminous board was Mars, trailing behind her two faint specks in space, one larger and brighter than the other. That was Deimos, the nearest source of water.

A crawling green point of light inched its way deliberately across the wide face of the board, ever dragging itself nearer to Mars and her two satellites. I put my finger on the green spot.

"The *Sprite*," I said slowly. "Are you getting everything out of her, Haj?"

Something of life flickered in his tired gray face. He rather worshipped his engines.

"I think—yes, I'm thinking we'll be able to pull a bit more from those engines, sir. If any engines can do it—"

I shook him affectionately, impatiently.

"I know *you'll* do it, man."

And then: "Good night, sir."

The engineer took himself off down the dark well leading below. But I felt little urge to sleep. Far from it. My head was a broiling mass of turmoil, swinging in a blind circle—there were so many things to be done, so many difficulties to face, so many problems to be grappled, if we were to win to Mars with a crippled ship and a decimated crew. But if it were possible, I swore it should be done.

I did not care so much about going out myself. After all, why should I? I had lived, thrilled, experienced things beyond the ordinary ken of man; and they say that Death is the Great Adventure. But I could not think only of myself; there were the men, who held to life with a tenacious grasp, and Haj, who still wanted greatly to live. I had to think of them.

I strapped myself finally into the control seat, prepared for a sleepless all-night watch, though there was in reality but little that I could do. Emergency automatic controls kept the ship tightly centered in the Jupiter Insulation Beam, swung her swiftly from the path of approaching meteorites.

The ship's clock burred and struck. I glanced at it, started incredulously. It was only one o'clock, ship chronometer time! So much had happened in that one hour since midnight!

In the observation-plates the heavens glittered with the ice-dust of uncounted stars. Mars glinted very faintly near the giant bright corona of the sun. And Earth—Earth was an almost invisible green sparkle in space, far distant, aloof, but still very beautiful.

I lost myself in the ever-fascinating wonder of it. The clock whirred sleepily. I caught myself nodding. I think I must have dozed....

CHAPTER III
Radium!

I TOOK my eye quickly from the viewpiece of the *Sprite's* single electro-telescope, and spoke into the engine-room speaking-tube. My voice was very hoarse and thick with thirst, but the welcome sight of the barren little planet swimming in the space ahead, with its promise of water, gave me a madman's strength.

"Deimos dead ahead!" I shouted wildly. "Prepare for landing! Forward beams reverse half-power! Aft beams cut off! Crew to landing-stations! Move!"

Below me, the thirst-mad crew wrestled insanely with the ponderous manuals of the forward photon-beams. Compressors throbbed a sullen song of power, groaned under the overload of hard-straining engines. The steelite shell of the ship, triple-braced as it was, quivered gently with the vibration.

And above in the control-room, I watched fierce streamers of released photons burst hotly from liquid captive light into free energy. The gigantic recoil slowed the ship perceptibly in her eager rush toward the approaching satellite.

I hesitated, hardly daring to use full power with the forward engines half-crippled from Jupiter warp. But the *Sprite's* velocity was far too great for safe landing.

"Full power all forward beams!" I shouted into the tube, casting caution to the winds.

The trembling black needles of the pressure gauges swung far over. Hot light gushed from the beam nozzles, backrushed soundlessly into the engine-room, filled the control cabin with the indefinable acrid sweetness of bursting light. Bright glowing plumes reached out far ahead of the quivering *Sprite*.

The light-ship dropped slowly down upon the scarred face of the dead satellite.

The valley was a nightmare in stone. Twisted masses of black rock covered the floor of a dust-thick plain that looked as though nothing had disturbed its utter barrenness since primeval ages. Alpine peaks weirdly like the jagged broken teeth of some gigantic stone animal walled in two sides of the canyon, which was shaped into rough semblance of a natural triangle. And finally, closing in the valley's mouth with a rampart of glowing ebony rock, lay the Man's Head peak—Man's Head and the Pool of eerie fire.

I saw the Pool first when I came out into the blinding sun-glare of the dust flats, garbed grotesquely in space-suit and quartz helmet, equipped with direction-finding instruments for locating the ship's bearings with regard to the Black Well. I had taken my observations upon the distant jutting peak that marked the Mountain of the Well, plotted our subsequent course in my mind's eye, and had turned to go back within the *Sprite*. Then something swung my head round as if it were set on an invisible pivot, and sent my eyes straight glancing toward the monstrous Head, with its crown of brightness.

The Mountain was formed of purest black rock, a dull satin sheened substance. It was un-Earthly in the slow fires that seemed to burn just below its murky surface, almost like a reflection of the Pool at its top. It was shaped into a mad caricature of a giant's monstrous head, with a gaping canyon slit for the great mouth, two pitted black craters for shadowed eyes, an outjutting promontory of jet rock formed into a foul travesty of a nose, and a pendulous drop of alabaster white for chin. I shuddered at that chin; in some indefinable fashion it twisted the whole shape of the Titan mouth into a cruel cold smile; turned the pitted eyes into the empty orbs of a monster skull; made the curve of the hawk nose ruthless and predatory. The thought was to come to me later that this Head had foreseen what my discovery of the Pool was to bring, the madness and stupidity it was to lead men into. But I had no inkling at the time.

My eyes swept up that gigantic face wrought in stone until they rested in stunned amazement on the burst of witches' light at its crown. Then something of insane fascination took hold on me, gripped my senses madly, lost me in a spinning maze of wildest sensation. The Pool was a molten lake of eca-radium!

It took no fluorescent screen or scientific knowledge to tell me that. The perfect fires that had their being at the summit of the Head flung the stunning fact almost in my face. The glinting brightness of that silver molten lake sent a slow madness creeping in my dazed brain.

But I managed, with a deliberate effort, to tear my eyes away. The Pool—this perfect lake of eca-radium, that valuable derivative of radium, was mine by right of priority. I was the first of all the myriads of the three worlds to lay my eyes upon it. And I was rich, rich beyond all dreams of avarice! Earth, I swore then, should be rich with me; I would give her power that should make her the greatest of the sun's planets. I would wipe out cancer. I would—

Slowly I forced myself back to reality. There were yet boundaries to be staked, possession claims yet to be made and entered in the Recording Office at Korna before I could call the Pool mine.

I half-ran back to the *Sprite*, roused a phlegmatic and indifferent Haj, burdened the two of us with a pile of luminous stake-markers, and began the monumental task of encircling the Pool with an unbreakable ring of possession claims.

Half-stumbling, half-walking, half-crawling on our knees over sharp-pointed slides of jagged rock, panting with an almost unbearable thirst, sweating beneath the load of our armor, we labored at the task for three unforgettable hours, carefully keeping our faces averted from the siren brightness of the Pool. But at last the job was done. We were very confident that our claims were now impregnable, incontestable. We were wrong.

I was standing back content, wiping the dust from the visor of my helmet, when Haj clutched suddenly at my arm, and spoke.

"Look there, sir!" he cried hoarsely, pointing. "A Martian!

Warship too, by the look of her! We're in for it now, sir!"

I felt inclined to agree with his pessimism, but still I was insanely confident, holding to my faith in the priority of claims. The Martian vessel, a lithe rakish light space cruiser, had sighted us and was swinging down rapidly over the nearer foothills. In ten minutes she had landed, opened a side port, and disembarked a party of three men, attired like ourselves in suits, but bearing upon the gilded crests of their steelite-rimmed helmets the insignia of the Royal Space Fleet of Mars.

They came toward us slowly, casting curious, suspicious glances upon our glinting ring of claim-markers. And suddenly one of them, a tall, bearded fellow of commanding aspect and with a more elaborate insignia than his friends, grasped his companions' arms and gestured excitedly, pointed upward, I could guess what he was saying.

My heart pounded unaccountably. An ominous foreboding of disaster throbbed a warning in my brain. They had discovered the Pool, that much was obvious. What course of action they would take—

They came climbing up the jagged rocks toward us. The tall man called:

"What ship is that? What's your business here?"

His voice had an iron ring. I waited until they had come up with us; then, calmly:

"We are from Earth, Commander. Commercial cargo-ship *Sprite*, Terrestrial registered. We were Korna-bound from Jupiter, but an accident destroyed our water apparatus three days back, forcing us to land here to take on a supply. You can look over our papers if you wish, though I assure you they're all in order."

He seemed oddly hesitant, uncertain of himself. He cast a glance at the two others, who were young, handsome, evidently not far removed from cadet days. Finally:

"We'll look over your papers, Earthman. There has been too much synthecholic smuggling from Jupiter's trading posts lately. No offense intended."

I bowed stiffly, and led the way down the rock slope to the *Sprite*. The lock door was open. I motioned the three Martians in ahead of myself and Haj, and after some little hesitation they obeyed. I closed the outside panel and started the air pumps. Seconds later, we stepped over the threshold of the lock.

The Martian scarcely looked at the *Sprite's* papers. Instead, he kept glancing in a queer manner around the room, peered down the stair well into the engine-room, rapped gingerly against the walls of the control-room, and in general conducted himself so strangely that his companions stared at him in amazement.

Suddenly he whirled round on me.

"Your papers, they are good, yes. That is so. But your men are very thirsty, eh, Captain? They would like water?"

Haj made a queer choking sound. I suppose my desire must have shown all too plainly in my eyes, for he nodded, chuckled. Then his cunning face drew into grave lines.

"My ship—it has too much water. Yes. An over-supply, so much that my men, though they drink much, cannot hope to drink it all. It is good, sweet, fresh water. Very good! Yes."

He paused. Haj was panting like a half-mad animal. I could hear the men cursing weakly at the bottom of the engine-room spiral. Staring at him, I said angrily:

"Are you trying to torture us? Out with it! What is it you want from me?"

But I knew. I knew! He looked at me with cunning eyes. He said very smoothly and softly:

"Ah, the good captain will not allow his men to suffer from the so-great thirst when there is water in plenty to be had; that is so, eh?"

To myself, I cursed him. But outwardly I smiled and nodded, matched his smoothness with my own.

"Yes, Commander," I said swiftly, "I will see that my men have water. We shall get it in plenty at the Black Well, which is near here I believe."

His lips tightened. Muffled anger was in his voice, but I could have sworn that deep back in his strange eyes was a sardonic glint of contemptuous laughter, almost as though he was playing with me. He said:

"But why, my friend, should you go so far for water, when my ship has it to overflowing? You shall not! No! *I* will give you all you need!"

I watched him warily, unheeding the cheer that rose from the parched throats in the room below and came hoarsely from the pallid lips of Haj. I said, very slowly:

"At what price?"

He hesitated, with again that curious uncertainty that I had noted before, as if he was dubious of the attitude of his companions. One of them, I was certain, was not behind him, for the young officer flung me a glance of encouragement and support. But the other—he was thin-faced, with cruel, sensuous lips. I did not like him. He glanced now full at the Commander, and nodded very slightly.

The big man said in a soft voice:

"All the water you shall want, if you but give up your impossible claims to this radium mountain! If you do not—" He shrugged; smiled. "Or here says that he found a quantity of synthecholic in your locker, my friend. And you will get no water...."

I stared angrily at Or, the younger officer, who was smiling unpleasantly. "I am allowed that amount for medicinal purposes, sir! How do you make out that I am a smuggler?"

Or shrugged indifferently. "We cannot judge, Captain. But we will be forced to hold you for the Court of Korna's investigation; that is, if you do not agree to the Commander's very fair proposal."

I turned from him, looked down over the stair-rail at the sullen, half-rebellious faces of the men. I shouted at them:

"Do you agree to let these brigands rob Earth of what is rightfully hers by authority of first discovery? Will you sell a world's ransom for a pittance of water? The Well of Deimos is not an hour's travel away; if it's water you want, we can get it there in plenty! What do you say?"

Their faces mirrored a racking struggle of conflicting emotions: thirst against titanic riches. Earth's call won. They shouted defiantly, swarming up the stairway:

"We'll stick with *you*, Chief! Throw these yellow-bellies out of here!"

Mingled surprise and anger flooded across the cruel faces of Or and the Commander; the young Cadet, anxiety on his clean features, jerked at their elbows, pointing at the inner lock panel. They shook him off, cursing. Or was grabbing for the para-gun slung at his hip.

"Cut that!" I shouted angrily, unwilling to see them massacre unarmed men. I swung the stellite hook of my space suit hard against his ugly chin. He dropped like a pole-axed ox, carrying the spitting Commander with him.

I heard a gasp from the younger officer. He looked at me queerly, whispered:

"Get their para-guns!"

I darted to the struggling heap of clashing metal bodies which represented the two fallen Martians, and jerked the deadly little paralytic weapons from their snug suit-holsters. I tossed them to the younger officer, who hastily secreted them in his armor.

The Commander and Or staggered erect at the instant my men from below came pouring up from the stairway. I stepped between the two hostile parties.

To the men: "Stay where you are!" To the Martian Captain and Or: "I think you see, gentlemen, that your proposal was not accepted!"

They glared at me. The Commander husked, swinging on the motionless younger officer: "Why didn't you attack when you saw us go down? This is treason!"

The younger man looked blank. "But, sir, what would you? I am disarmed!"

He showed his empty para-holster, gestured helplessly.

The Commander looked mollified at that. He turned his anger to me.

"What do you mean by this? By A-taz, I'll have you before the High Court of Korna for this madness!"

I regarded him coolly. I motioned one arm.

"Move," I said, my eyes on his. "Leave this ship. We owe you no allegiance; we are Terrestrial only. Go, and remember that our claims are first on the mountain of radium here!"

I had forgotten Or. The next I knew of him came with a wild shout from Haj:

"Sir! Look out!—Behind you!"

I half-turned, swung out blindly, and felt something descend with stunning force on my head. I sank into black oblivion....

CHAPTER IV
Treachery!

WHEN I came again to consciousness Haj was bending solicitously over me, chafing my wrists and rubbing my hot forehead with cool hands. I stared up at him in a daze, only half remembering what had befallen. Then full reason returned, and I sat up, felt gingerly of a swelling lump on the back of my head.

Haj told me that Or had come up behind while I was haranguing the Martian Commander, and struck me over the head with the clubbed arm of his metal suit. I had dropped like one dead, and the three Martians, supposedly unarmed, had beaten a hasty retreat before the vengeful onslaught of the crew. The younger officer, in his hurry, had dropped a thermos flask of water from his armor before vanishing through the lock.

The crew since had somewhat quenched their thirst, and had given evidence of even being willing to go on to Mars without touching the Well, in order that we might lay our claims to the Pool in Korna before the Martians.

Haj said that they had paid no more attention to the *Sprite*, but through glasses he had observed activity aboard the Martian ship, and shortly a party of spacemen came out from the ship, destroyed with ruthless thoroughness all traces of our claim-stakes, and began laying down a wall of steelite about the Man's Head. A squad of green-helmeted ground troops was posted at spaced intervals along the Wall, armed with rapid-firing para-guns and Ehz-Ta grenade throwers.

And later in the three hours that I had lain unconscious in the *Sprite*, as the small red sun dropped closer to the horizon, a forward torpedo tube was trained by the Martian on the *Sprite*. A gun crew clustered grimly about it, tensed, waiting. And an officer in scarlet and with a bandaged jaw paced impatiently along the observation deck behind the menacing tube-gun, glancing now and again at the glinting face of some small object strapped to his wrist. He looked often at the fading orb of the weak sun.

"I think it means they intend to fire on us, sir," said Haj, and added as an apparent afterthought: "The one called Or shouted something to us as he left; sounded like '—we'll give you till sundown. After that—' I couldn't get the rest of it."

Realization stung my brain. For the first time I was able to believe that the warship actually meant to fire on the hapless *Sprite*. I sprang up, lashing Haj with a fusillade of orders that sent him hurrying down the engine-room spiral to rouse the crew to action. Fighting a nauseating weakness that gripped my splitting head, I strapped myself in haste to the control-seat.

And shortly I heard below the muffled throbbing of strained compressors, the faint soft hiss of swirling photon-beams, the subdued clatter of moving beam-manuals. I sat hunched in the bucket-seat of the control-seat, eyes tight and straining upon the wavering finger of the light-pressure needle. Slowly, so slowly that my heart pounded a frantic tattoo in my temples and despair ate into my brain, did that accursed needle creep around the impassive face of the luminous dial.

The last thin crimson splash of the distant tepid sun bathed the dial in weird red light. I saw it: take-off pressure at last! I shouted hoarsely, half-madly, into the engine-room tube. Beneath me the engines bellowed, and light swirls leaped full-born in mad flashing from hot beam-nozzles,—and the *Sprite* shook the age-old dust of the plain from her fleet heels and rushed wildly upward into the black curtain of the sky. Faint, far below, I caught the baffled flash of the warship's fire.

But we were away, and in the clear. Mars ho! I grabbed the speaking-tube in an exultant grip and asked Haj for more power. The engines responded in a sweet song of sobbing strength, strength—and speed. And speed it was that we needed most.

I watched the dial-needles and prayed for more velocity. There was little doubt but that the warship would follow us. That officer I had felled, Or, thick-headed as he was, would most certainly realize the all-importance of first-claims. If I could but lay my case before the Recording Office at Korna, before he followed, then the Pool was mine!

I swung the telescope to focus behind the speeding *Sprite*. A silver needle was lancing out from the dark scarred surface of Mars' dead moon, and leaping after us with a certain indomitable doggedness. I shivered a little, felt a quake of wild fear. That wardog, despite the overwhelming lead we'd had, was most certainly overtaking us!

Overtaking us! The words had the ring of doom to my ears. For the *Sprite* was straining her sweet engines already to the utmost limits of their power; a little more, and the overload would finish them. We were helpless; there was nothing I could do to stave off the defeat that came leaping up from behind.

Half-sobbing with mingled anger and black despair, I watched that grim lance of silver flame that was the Martian leap swiftly upon the failing *Sprite*, draw even, and then pass us! There was no sign of hostility from her, for out here were the wide traffic-lanes for passenger-liners and Earth freighters. The war vessel did not quite dare to destroy an unarmed ship so openly.

I caught a glimpse of my enemy, the bearded Commander, through the glassite covering of the bridge as the battle cruiser slipped past, and finally left us far behind. He gave me a mocking, sardonic bow.

I think it hardly made impression. I had already plumbed the uttermost depths of black despair.

Of course I stood no chance when my appeal came before the High Court of the Korna district. The facts lay very plain. The Martian Commander was all in the right, and I was all in the wrong—simply a usurper, a brigand, altogether a perjured villain.

The Chief of Korna's Recording Office testified glibly against me, and on cross-examination produced his records and showed that the patriotic Commander had forewarned him against my brigandage. I turned half-sick at that. The subtle irony of the man!

But still I held a trump card in the hole. And finally, in desperation I played it. Films. Thin strips of metal tape, upon which were recorded images of certain Martian officers ordering the destruction of my claim-stakes, substituting Martian markers in their place, then setting up a guard over the Head and the Pool. Films that Haj, luckily had had the supreme wit to take with the *Sprite's* single recording camera.

The Court-Hall, at the command of the judges, was darkened. Haj and a Martian officer-of-the-court who had knowledge of camera-operation went into a small booth set at the far end of the room, and began to prepare the portable projection apparatus kept there. I could see the sudden blanched faces of two of the three officers, who sat together in a close group. One of them—I think it was Or—stirred, and whispered urgently to his companions. One objected violently, but the other nodded and quelled the dissenter with a look. I swear that that one slipped a tiny glinting vial from his uniform, and concealed it in the shadow that lay about him.

The films began. A blur at first, gray, distorted, wavering. Then giving way to the bare dusty desolation of the valley floor, showing clearly the small figures of two Martian officers, long thin lines of moving soldiery. The officers were shouting commands—

Something hurtled across the dark room and splattered against metal. The images on the silver screen vanished abruptly. I caught Haj's angry exclamation.

The lights flashed on. And in the projection-room Haj and the operator stared blankly at the crumbling wreck of the projecting machine. Acid fumes bit at the white metal, licked hungrily at the thin spool of the film tape caught at its centre.

Grim-faced, Haj thrust a thin bare arm down into that swirling deadly mist and gripped the little roll of record tape. He tore it from its fastenings by main strength, brought his arm up in an arc, flung the film away. It lit, rolled, came slowly to a stop.

I picked it up. The acid had touched. Not much certainly. But still, I knew, enough to ruin the value of those films as legal evidence. I shoved the metal spool inside my cloak, forced a smile, and gripped Haj's hand. He grinned at me, choking down the evident torture of his burned arm.

"The film is safe, yes?" he asked eagerly.

"Of course, Haj," I lied. "Great work! But you've got to have treatment for that arm. Off you go. Don't worry. I can handle the rest of this myself. You've won for us. You'll go, now."

He hesitated, staring at me. Then he saluted, went off in the solicitous company of two attendants. I swung round on the gaping judges.

"That is all of my case."

One of the Martian officers laughed unpleasantly. He gestured to his companions. I knew the meaning of that gesture. He was right. Earth had lost the Pool.

I almost wish now that I had let it stand at that. If I had known what was to come, how near the Pool would bring

Earth and Mars to conflict, I might have. But as it was, I could not be content. I carried the fight to New Washington.

Leaving Haj to recover from the almost disastrous effects of his acid-burns in the comfortable surroundings of the Terrestrial Hospital at Korna, I took passage on the first space-liner leaving the port for Earth's Capitol. And once in Washington, I went straight to the World Secretary of State.

I faced him in a small bare room in a certain unobtrusive section of the Greater Capital, and laid my cards on the table. I had brought the damaged films with me.

The Secretary received my story calmly—and skeptically. But that big man has a keen mind, an open, unbiased intellect. He demanded proof. I showed him the package of films.

He took them thoughtfully, with something of his skepticism vanishing, and remarked that he knew a certain man in the line of films who would be eager to see what could be done with mine. I was told to come back in a week.

I came. At the end of the week prescribed, I sat again opposite the Secretary of State. He looked thoughtfully across at me from behind small round windows of lens-glass and many layers of fat. I do not believe you know him, Grant. But he is a very fat man, the Secretary, very indolent-looking, very jovial. Appearances are deceiving. For the eyes almost buried in the thick lines of flesh around his high cheek-bones are, if you look closely, queerly clear and piercing. The real intelligence of the man is evident in their bright quick depths.

"Diplomacy," said the Secretary after a long silence, "is a very ticklish business, Gray. When you try to convince a Martian who thinks you're doubtless some sort of irrational beast, that you've got something he needs, and that he should exchange for it with you something he doesn't want but you need, then you go beyond the safer realms of human diplomacy. It's devil-take-the-hindmost. It almost looks as though we're the hindmost this time, Gray. You've gotten us into a perfect devil of a mess.

"Mars needs that radium. But she can get along without it. Earth absolutely can't. We've wasted, and wasted, until radium's about the only thing we've got to fall back on. If we're not able to tap that Pool of yours, Gray, within the next three years, then we're finished."

He stared at me. "Earth will be through as a Great Power.... Understand?"

I nodded, a little shocked. He hesitated. Finally:

"Now. Those films of yours, Gray, have been developed, projected before the President, the Cabinet, myself, and the Commanders of our Army and Spatial Navy. They've convinced the Government of the justice of your claims.

"We've told Boma that Earth intends to lay title to the Man's Head and the Pool. And—this is confidential—the light cruiser *Falcon,* Captain Lanson commanding, has taken over the Mountain in the name of the Terrestrial Government."

He stared at me hard, hesitating. Then:

"Boma, as official Ambassador from Mars, has given us his ultimatum. These are its terms: Withdraw the *Falcon;* acknowledge our claims as absolutely false; proclaim you an outlaw, a brigand, an unvarnished pirate with a price on your head.

"And if we don't yield to those impossible terms—well, Boma is a secret member of the Martian United War Party. He means war. He wants war. He thinks that old Mars, strong and toughened by her eternal battle for survival, must take a younger, weaker Earth for her own.

"Of course, we refused his ultimatum. Refused, and saw him go aboard the battle cruiser he's had waiting in port the last three days, headed hell-bent for Mars. He'll go straight to the Red Emperor, and ask for war with Earth. Most probably, he'll get it.

"But we've still, Gray, one chance for peace. Earth will offer Mars free of charge our secret for producing water synthetically. She has always paid us an indemnity for its use. Now we'll trade it for all Martian rights to the Mountain and the Pool. With unlimited water Mars will be young again, won't need that radium.

"Here's Earth's official proposal. Recorded this morning by the World President, in the presence of myself and the members of the Cabinet. If you can reach the Red Throne at Korna before Boma, we'll still have a chance for peace.

"You must, Gray! There's a Star liner leaving Grand Central Space Terminal at twelve tonight; the *Trident.* She's fast, a crack Mars ship. Faster than Boma's cruiser, the *Breemoor.*

If you board the *Trident* tonight—"

I nodded. My head was throbbing.

"I will, sir."

He passed a small messenger's pouch, sealed, across the table. He studied me a minute with those lancet eyes, and, suddenly grinning, stretched a firm hand to meet mine.

"Bon voyage, Gray!"

I saluted him, thrust the sealed pouch under my arm, and was gone.

CHAPTER V
War!

GRAY'S voice stopped. The captain looked at him, and said thoughtfully:

"A leak somewhere. Korna Intelligence got wind of your mission. And put a man aboard here—to stop you. That explains the episode of the zina."

Gray nodded. He was grave.

"Yes, I think so. But, look here, Grant, I've kept you up far too long as it is. I'd better be getting back to my own cabin. You need your sleep."

The captain ignored the words. He said:

"Got a question. Ever noticed anything wrong in your cabin after you'd been away awhile? Evidence of search, I mean. Little things. A disarrangement of the room, a scratch on your baggage that wasn't there before—"

Gray knit his brows in thought. He frowned.

"Right. Now that you mention it, I remember being troubled several times with an odd belief that something in my room had been changed in my absence. When I'd come back from dinner or a deck stroll, I'd find certain things I couldn't lay a name to. Things wrong with the arrangement of my cabin. They must have searched it often, looking for the pouch."

The captain nodded.

"Yes. If I'm not too curious, where *do* you keep it?"

Gray patted his arm-pit significantly.

"Right here under my shoulder. And I've got a Bressler under the other arm. Oh, I was pretty well prepared for the ordinary; but that zina—I hadn't counted on that."

The captain's eyes lit up suddenly.

"Gray! These Martians! What if they should declare a state of war with Earth? We'd simply cut off the insulation beams, and they'd be pretty helpless. Surely they haven't—"

He stopped, sudden horror in his eyes. Gray smiled a little wryly.

"They have. A little over a month ago the Patent Offices in the War Building at Washington were entered and robbed of the blue-prints for the Ostler Insulation Beam. The thieves were traced to the Ambassador's Palace of the Martian Colony; the investigators from the State Department didn't dare go any farther."

Grant stared at him. There was a silence. Gray broke it with a protest that he should be returning to his own cabin. The words brought the captain out of a brown study. He said indignantly:

"Haven't you just told me that whoever's hunting your scalp has as much entry to your cabin as you have? That upper bunk's perfectly useless, Gray. You're staying here."

And Gray yielded, under protest. In five minutes he had divested himself of his clothes, said good night, and climbed into the vacant bunk. In ten minutes he was sleeping soundly.

The captain looked up at him in admiration.

"What a nerve!" he whispered, and went to bed.

The party in the dining salon broke up at one and Grant, making his excuses, took a solitary way back to his sleeping-cabin, leaving Gray to follow on more slowly with an intriguing feminine acquaintance he had made.

The captain walked presently down a deserted stretch of corridor that ended in a dark, shadow-filled deck-corner. Remembering his experience of the night before he approached the corner warily, cast a searching glance into the vagueness—and with an abrupt motion flattened himself in the shadows.

He was very near an unshuttered look-out plate upon which was mirrored the silent black and white pageant of the stars. A white tongue of light had just licked swiftly across that black sky curtain. He strained his eyes for a second glimpse.

It came again. A regular spacing. Flash. Short flash. Long flash. Flash. A code, spelling out words that were meaningless to Grant. Flash. Flash.

He strove to locate in his mind the direction of that flashing. That it was somewhere on the ship he knew, but just where.... He'd struck it. From the helio-room, of course!

But the thought stiffened him. There was a night operator on duty always in the signal room, and certainly none of the *Trident's* men would be sending in a strange code—especially at this time of "Night." It meant that the operator was not on duty....

He thrust aside the idea that the signal man had deserted his post. He knew that the man was loyal, fully conscious of the fact that there must always be someone on watch in the helio-room. Someone must watch for the flickering of distress signals from some other ship that might need the urgent help of the giant liner, and if unheeded might slip slowly into the limbo of missing ships—the unimaginable maelstrom of free space.

The operator had been overcome. That, Grant felt certain, was the answer. And someone was signaling. Flash. Flash. Flash. Flash. He pressed himself against the look-out plate, glanced behind the path of the speeding liner. And suddenly he saw it: a far-off wavering speck of light. Light that came and vanished, flickered dully. A distant helio. Sending now. Flash. Flash. Flash.

Gibberish to Grant. Clever code! He tried to penetrate its hidden meaning, and failed. Flash. Flash. Flash. The thought came to him that the operator would need him. That unknown signaler must not slip through him.

Like a star shell, the identity of the night signaler came in a burst to him. Gray's enemy, the K. I. agent! Korna Intelligence! Signaling....

A sudden feeling of disaster grew in him. The signaling meant danger to the *Trident*, he was abruptly sure. He had to stop it. Cautiously, he moved up the ramp leading to the helio ladder.

Slow, silent progress along the ramp to the foot of the narrow stellite ladder. Light streamed from under the door at the top. But no sound came now from the sealed helio cabin. The signaling had stopped, and abruptly, the light vanished.

Grant's spine prickled a little. In the thick gloom of the ramp, he strained his eyes for the darker shape of the cabin door above. It opened, and shadows swirled thickly an instant about it.

A vague black figure came down the ladder like a scuttling dark spider, and flashed past him. He whirled, struck out vainly with futile fists, lurched forward in the darkness, and sprawled upon the hard smooth metal of the ramp floor. The K. I. had won again. He listened for the soft mockery of laughter.

It did not come. And he realized abruptly that the conflict between Gray and himself and the unknown had tightened, changed from a sardonic game into a grim battle of life and death. Something had come insidiously across space in those night signals. A cold something, that penetrated icily into the *Trident's* vitals. Grant muttered to himself.

He became conscious of dragging movement in the cabin above him, a thumping sound across the metal floor that ended as suddenly as it had begun. Light flashed in the cabin again. And Grant moved with caution up the ladder, flung open the closed door, and entered.

Everything looked much as usual, save that the helio operator, sitting forward in his bucket-seat, seemed to wear an odd look of dazed bewilderment. But he saluted smartly enough at the captain's entry. Grant stared at him.

"What happened to you?"

The operator rubbed his head in a kind of vague bewilderment. He said slowly: "What happened to me! Why, sir, has—"

"Listen," Grant interrupted him. "Someone has been signaling in a foreign code from this room for the past half hour. How did they knock you out? Or did they?"

The operator looked at him rather pleadingly. He said at last:

"Don't know if you'll believe me or not sir, but I can swear I was sitting here like this a little while ago, everything just as usual, when of a sudden some creepin' sort of white mist-stuff comes seeping under the edge of the door, and whirls across the floor toward me. It got to me, billowed up around my face, and I felt kind of choky and sleepy and warm, and I had a feeling that somebody wanted me to go to sleep. I don't remember a thing after that, sir. Next thing I saw was you."

Grant knew when he was up against a blank wall. There was nothing more to be got from this man. He shook the other by the shoulder and warned him:

"I believe you. But I wouldn't try to convince anyone else with that story if I were in your place. Just forget it. And tell Mr. Hallton that an air-tight door should be put in here as soon as possible in the morning. We want no more of this. You'll have your own oxygenation apparatus. Good night."

The man saluted gratefully.

"Good night, sir."

Grant went down the ladder. He made a brisk way of the short walk to the sleeping-cabin, found the door locked, and entered with his key. He had not expected Gray to be there. Gray had seemed quite taken with the beautiful Martian, Edda Me-Tor. He must warn him about that.

The captain had divested himself of most of his warm uniform and was in the process of entering his bunk when Gray, whistling a gay tune, swung open the cabin door and came briskly in. Grant hid his grin.

"Did you see her all the way to her room, Gray?" he asked solemnly. Gray flung him a suspicious glance.

"Who do you mean? Edda? Why, no I didn't. She insisted on leaving me at about the first turn in the corridor. But she promised to take a deck stroll with me after breakfast tomorrow, so—" He made a little gesture. But Grant's wicked smile had faded. He was sitting on the edge of the bunk, watching Gray gravely.

With a sudden imperious motion for silence, he launched tersely into a report of the night's happenings. Gray heard him out.

"Looks rather like the K. I. people haven't given up getting me yet, doesn't it?" he said soberly. "If this keeps up, I'll be hiring you as a permanent bodyguard, Grant."

"Yes," said Grant rather absently, "You'll have to be careful." And then: "You say she wouldn't let you take her all the way to her cabin, eh?"

Gray stared at him, stopped the progress of his undressing.

"What do you mean?"

"Nothing," Grant said looking away. "Nothing. Only— she's Martian, you know, and a member of the highest Circle.

Just a friendly warning, Gray."

"Thanks," said Gray dryly. "I'll keep it in mind."

Over breakfast the next morning in the salon, the talk at the captain's table was mainly of the party the night before, and both Grant and Gray were content to keep it in that channel. Grant spoke very little, keeping his eyes on his plate when they were not watching Gray with a slight worried frown. He did not like the spell that the Martian Edda had seemed to cast over the Earthman.

Gray was not as troubled by Grant's story of the night before as he would have been a day previously, because he was very much absorbed in the conversation of the girl across the table from him. Her eyes and lips sparkled when she spoke in a low husky voice like some ancient fermented wine.

Gray thought that she was by far the most interesting woman at the captain's table, and certainly the most beautiful. She was. Small, and quick, and clean-lined, with a pensive, intelligent face, and the alluring eyes of some elfin goddess.... Others in the captain's party had already lost their heads to her: Tauro, the Venusian nobleman, a talented cynic and aristocrat.... Marchman, the middle-aged traveling representative for Interplanetary Trading Co.... Ehta, a slim young Martian boy, who worshipped her as a beautiful goddess, and who was the son of one of Korna's great titled houses, a member of the Upper Circle of Mars.

But all of them had regretfully conceded first place in her flickering affections to John Audley, the Terrestrial commercial artist (for such Gray was posing to be), though of that fact Audley had little or no inkling. He was certain that she liked him. Little side glances that were flung his way, the soft intonation of the husky wine-tinted voice when she bantered sparkling repartee with him across the table, the look in her dark elfin eyes—all told him that at least. But he did not know how much she liked him, if somewhere in her affections friendship ended and love began. That he would have desired fervently to know, but always she kept it skilfully from him, baffling, angering, teasing, overcoming him when he pressed her with a flurry of devastating banter.

He knew that she fascinated him. Fascinated, and a little more. It was very hard to analyze his exact feelings toward her. Often there was sheer attraction, lure, a whirling maelstrom of queer emotion. And often—a slight hesitation, a feeling of half-doubt that was almost a warning to stay away, when he struck well-hidden notes of ice buried under the warm exterior.

Tauro was speaking, leaning across the table:

"What do you think, Meta* Edda, of this controversy between Earth and your planet over those mines of Deimos? I think myself this Gray is an unprincipled brigand. The word of a Martian officer is not to be so lightly taken as these Earthlings seem to think."

She wrinkled her clear brows thoughtfully.

"I do not know. That Gray—he tries so hard, seems so very much in earnest. It is hard to believe such a one a brigand. And yet—I know that the officers of the Majesty's Fleet are gentlemen. They do not lie, no. I—I think there must be misunderstanding somewhere, something that we onlookers do not know."

Tauro applauded mockingly, laughing.

"Bravo, Edda! You are most fair. Very fair! Isn't she, my dear Audley?"

Gray in his role of Audley answered carefully:

"Very fair, friend Tauro. She is very wise, Meta Edda. Almost, shall we say, almost as wise as she is beautiful."

A quick murmur of applause went round the table, while Edda flushed fascinatingly and uttered deprecating words. She was saying something to Tauro when Grant tugged urgently at Gray's right sleeve. The captain was rising. A starch-coated steward, very pale, stood waiting at Grant's elbow. Grant said:

"You will excuse us, please. We will return in a moment."

Gray, thinking with regret of his after-breakfast appointment with Edda, got up reluctantly and followed at the captain's heels. Grant was looking very grave. He dismissed the white-faced steward at the bottom of the ladder going up into the control-room and took Gray's arm, spoke in a low voice:

"We've sighted a Martian warship about one thousand miles behind us, Gray. I think she means some sort of trouble. Doesn't answer our signals; and there is the business of last night to consider."

Gray sobered at once, his stroll forgotten.

---

*Meta. A title of respect, applied to feminine Martian nobility.

"You mean the K. I. man was signaling this warship?"

Grant nodded. They entered the control-cabin together and took a stand close to one of the great look-out plates. A tense atmosphere had invaded the crowded control-room. Brame, the second officer, turned a white strained face to them.

"She's coming up on us fast, sir. Must be making all the speed they've got. Shall I order more power in the compressors, sir? We can outrun her."

But Grant was stubborn. He shook his head.

"We'll have a talk with them first."

He glanced across the narrow catwalk between control- and helio-room. The signalman was on duty, alert, with an air of tenseness about him.

And suddenly a blinding flicker of light seared across the control-room. The helio snapped and jerked.

"Signaling us, Grant!" Gray said excitedly. The captain was silent, watching the furious fingers of the helio operator. Presently the man rose and passed the message across.

"ABOARD H. M. S. BREEMOR. TO THE COMMANDING OFFICER OF THE S. L. TRIDENT. MESSAGE FOLLOWS:

"STOP SHIP IMMEDIATELY. YOU ARE LAWFUL PRIZE OF WAR, AND AS SUCH WILL BE TAKEN BY FORCE IF NECESSARY. HOSTILITIES NOW EXIST BETWEEN OUR GOVERNMENTS. THE CONSEQUENCES OF ANY RESISTANCE WILL BE ON YOUR HEAD.—BOMA, COMMANDING, H. M. S. BREEMORE."

"Boma!" Gray cried. "It's Boma's ship! Do you see? The fool thinks we're already at war? What will you do, Grant?"

The captain, grim-faced was speaking tersely to the helioman. "Take this message:

"ABOARD STAR LINER TRIDENT. TO THE COMMANDING OFFICER OF H. M. S. BREEMOOR:

"SEE YOU IN HELL FIRST. THIS IS PIRACY! WILL REPORT YOUR ACTION TO THE INTERPLANETARY BOARD AT KORNA AT ONCE.—R. GRANT, COMMANDING, S. L. TRIDENT."

The helio swung and flickered. Gray noted the sudden increase of activity aboard the warship's decks. Guns swung swiftly round toward the defiant Trident. Gun crews took stations, clustered grimly about their shining weapons.

Green-helmeted boarding parties gathered in squadrons before the cruiser's exit-locks.

The Breemor was signaling again:

"OUR NATIONS ARE AT WAR. REPEAT YOU ARE LAWFUL PRIZE. LAST WARNING.—BOMA, COMMANDING, H. M. S. BREEMOOR."

And suddenly Gray shot across the narrow space of the control-cubby, grasped the *Trident's* beam-controls, and swung them far over. Grant gasped.

"A trick! To get our attention on the guns, while they try a hull shot with a forward projector-tube!"

The *Trident* was diving. Down, down, ever down. Almost to the far edge of the Insulation Beam, and then zooming as swiftly back again. The projector-bolt had shot on past the whirling liner, a hot licking tongue of bright flame.

"Torpedo!" Grant shouted into the speaking tube. A harsh whine came up from the bottom of the *Trident*, and a silver spinning object shot out from the liner's nose in a direct line for the warship. The *Breemoor* did not even deign to swerve. A perfectly aimed salvo from the forward guns, and the bright object burst into a mushroom of futile flame. That was the *Trident's* feeble gesture at resistance.

After that, contemptuous gunners aboard the Martian laid down a perfect barrage of electronic bolts about the hapless liner, ringing her with row after row of heat bursts that came close but did not touch her. The *Trident's* feeble armament could not even penetrate that barrier of energy. The fight was over. Grant knew it, and spoke bitterly to the white-faced helioman:

"Take this message. For the sake of the passengers, Gray:

"ABOARD THE TRIDENT. TO THE BREEMOOR. MESSAGE FOLLOWS:

"YOU WIN, DAMN YOU!—GRANT, COMMANDING, S. L. TRIDENT."

He did not look at Gray. They stood together, silent, bitter, sick with futile anger, while the *Trident's* engines slowed and died, leaving the ship curiously desolate and silent. The luminous tricolor of Earth faded with reluctance from the *Trident's* blunt prow.

The warship, triumphant, swung in closer to the *Trident*, and prepared for the debarkation of boarding parties. Gray could see the ordered excitement aboard the *Breemoor*, the swift marshaling of fierce-visaged green helmets, almost glimpse the victorious smiles of the ship's officers.... And suddenly, it was all gone, wiped away into nothingness.

A bright spinning object had leaped suddenly from the *Trident's* nose, bridged the narrow gap between warship and liner so swiftly that the *Breemoor* had no time to move, and struck. There came a fierce mushroom of yellow flame, a wild burst of flaring light—and the *Breemoor* had crumpled like a ship of cardboard, a child's toy that a giant's hand had smashed.

Gray, exultant, was pounding Grant's shoulder:

"Got her, Grant! By glory, you owe some torpedo man aboard this ship a vote of thanks! We've won, man!"

But Grant was curiously silent and grave. He said at last:

"But we'd surrendered, Gray. It was rather beastly to take them unaware like—that. We've violated our surrender."

Gray shook him a little.

"Did they hesitate because we had women and children aboard, passengers who couldn't fight?"

The captain's face hardened.

"No, by the Lord Harry, they didn't! The beasts!"

Gray shook his head gravely.

"No, Grant, not beasts. Just men—men at war."

Later, as they left the control-room together, Gray said thoughtfully:

"I wonder if Boma could have known about the pouch? Those signals...."

Grant looked speculative. He said:

"I wonder!"

CHAPTER VI
Midnight on Mars

GRAY stood watching the myriad sparkling lights that came rushing up to him from below. The *Trident* dropped down in a long smooth slant toward the great irregular splash of luminous glow that marked Korna Space Port. They had made Korna at last! Korna, first city of Red Mars!

The ship's announcers blared it in metallic monotones:

"Korna! All passengers who are debarking at Korna use exit-ports numbered Five, Six, and Seven; take places on Z-Deck. Baggage windows open now.... All passengers debarking at—"

There was a speaker blaring hoarsely directly above his head, but if he heard it, Gray gave no sign. He stood a slight figure in black, close by the hulking mechanism of an exit-lock, dark cloak caught loosely about him, eyes intent upon the open door across the deck through which the passengers debarking must come.

He had already looked through the crowd on the deck. Edda was not there. A glance had told him that: the crowd was small and thinly scattered on the wide deck-floor. There were not many debarking here. The ship's list this trip had been made up principally of commercial travelers with business in the great polar cities of Brez and Trela; not likely to debark here in quiet Korna, small city hanging close to the barrens of the Red Desert, unimportant in the widening circles of interplanetary business—but withal, a city of considerable power, as the ancient seat of Martian government.

Gray noted among the crowd a little group of power lobbyists gathered in a corner by themselves, a cold-eyed woman with a flurry of respectful servants and a harassed-looking male escort who was addressed as "Meta," a dowager duchess from a small Balkan Earth nation, making obviously a first visit to Mars; a sprinkling of debutantes voyaging to the Red Court of Mars, the chairman of a powerful South Martian Political Union—and the inevitable group of servile nonentities who attached themselves as opportunity offered. Nothing unusual here—it was a typical passenger-liner crowd.

Gray was waiting for Edda. She had told him that she was debarking here, rejoining her father after a long stay at a Terrestrial university. But so far she had not come. He hoped fervently that she would, and watched with impatience the changing glow of lights in the pilot's cabin—at red the door across the deck would swing closed, and the exit-locks be opened by spacemen.

The neon light flamed red. The door across began swinging slowly shut, at the same instant that a slight figure garbed in daring scarlet half-ran down the metal steps, slipped through the narrowing opening, and hurried breathlessly up to Gray.

"Oh, I have kept you waiting! I am sorry, Mr. Audley. You will forgive me, yes? But really I had no idea it was so late.... Why, think of it, I might have missed debarking! That would have been unbearable!"

"It would," Gray laughed, "for me."

She smiled at him approvingly. "Always you are the polite one, saying the right thing in the right place. Yes, I am glad that I was not too late to disembark with you. You must come with me to my father's house. He will most certainly want to meet you."

But there was a curious lack of warmth in the words. Almost insincerity. Gray could have sworn he caught a glint of moisture in the dark eyes. Afterwards he was to remember that tear, and know its meaning. But now he was puzzled, bewildered.

"Later, Meta Edda. First I must attend to this boresome business. I am to paint for one of your great ones. He would be difficult if I kept him waiting. But later—certainly."

She did not protest nearly as much as he wanted her to. A silence fell between them. Surreptitiously he studied her, watched the changing lights in her dark eyes, the soft rustle of her daring scarlet, the perfect curving of her half-parted lips. She was like some ancient, subtly-tinted painting, he thought. The exotic fascination of her alien beauty swept him again.

He was leaning forward to speak when the captain came hurrying up to where they stood. Grant was frowning a little. He bowed politely to Edda, and drew Gray off to one side.

"Careful there, old man. You're playing with a mighty dangerous brand of fire. And—you might get burnt." He shrugged expressively. Gray was half angry.

"Just a friendly warning?" he inquired softly, dangerous lights in his eyes. Grant gave him an almost pleading glance.

"Yes. Forget it if you want. And now—this other business." He hesitated. "I've got a man in the crowd watching for anything out of the ordinary. He'll stick near you. I don't believe K. I. is willing to quit yet. So—watch yourself."

Gray promised. The captain stood a moment in silence. Then: "And—good luck, Gray."

They shook hands warmly in the darkness. The captain spoke a last word and moved off with reluctance. Lights were blazing down now on the metal deck, springing into the fierce, almost dazzling glow of the great Terminal Luminors. The great ship dropped easily into the resilient grasp of a landing-cradle, came to rest with scarcely a jar.

Gray rejoined Edda by the lock mechanism. And presently a spaceman in the blue-and-white uniform of the Star Company came up to them, took the smooth wheels of the lock panels in his bronzed capable hands. The inner panel moved slowly, to the accompaniment of a subdued mechanical clicking.

Gray and Edda joined the thin stream of passengers pouring into the air-lock, a small square chamber, metal-walled, that jutted out from the rounded side of the ship. And presently the soft clicking behind them faded, stopped. The outer panel slid open.

Gray felt the soft rush of the ship's air moving past him into the lighter Martian atmosphere. He took a deep breath, and thrilled to an electric tingling. The gravity of Mars took hold on him. It was curiously small and ineffective, after the Earth Normal maintained in the ship. Edda swayed a little against him.

A queer feeling rose in him at her warm touch. His senses swirled; and then remembering Grant's warnings he steadied again. He moved away. The white-lit opening of the air-lock gaped before them. He took her arm politely, stepped out beside her on the top of the narrow steelite debarking-ladder that led down to the ground. The ship was nestled snugly in the high curving uprights of a landing-cradle.

The passenger-stream was in some confusion, seemed backing uncertainly upon itself. A babble of conflicting voices came from below, where the first of the line of debarkers were gathered. A little plump man encased in a smooth-fitting uniform covered with overmuch braid was haranguing the crowd. His insignia proclaimed the Port Officer of Korna.

Gray pushed a slow way for Edda and himself through the swirling confusion. They were near the foot of the landplank presently, listening to the final words of the little man:

"... Owing to strained relations between our respective

governments, I will be obliged to hold all of you until a decision on the matter can be given. This is an official order from the Palace, issued at midnight. All ships incoming from Earth are to be held."

Gray went cold. Strained relations! Then the possibility of open hostilities soon was very strong. If he could but reach the Palace of Gage, Earth ambassador to Mars, give his message of peace in time! He must.

Edda said suddenly, after a silence:

"Oh, this is impossible! I am going back to the ship, Mr. Audley. I will wait for you on the landing-deck. Surely this madness cannot last! I am sure Jan-Shawan will let us through before very long. I will wait for you. Come for me when we are allowed to disembark."

Without giving him opportunity to reply, she had gone. Gray looked after her in mingled bewilderment and regret. She would have to wait for him longer than she knew. He would have no time to return to the ship if Grant's ingenuity found a way through the port guards, as it must.

Someone brushed crushingly against him. He looked up with an angry exclamation on his lips, and caught the brusk nod of Grant's head. The captain had come hurriedly down the gang-plank. He was asking all passengers to return to the ship. And reluctantly, they were going. The crowd thinned.

Gray joined Grant and the little port officer at the foot of the landplank. The captain had evidently known the small man before. He said, pretending complete ignorance:

"What's this about, Jan-Shawan?"

The Martian was suddenly voluble. He burst into eager explanations.

"Madness, Captain, madness! This accursed radium they've found on a mountain of Deimos; the Palace and those stubborn-heads at Washington—always begging your pardon, sir—have almost come to war over it. There are rumors that Boma's left Earth and headed for the Throne, to ask for breaking off of relations with Earth. They're saying Korna Laboratories has discovered a new method of insulating light ships against the radiations of free space, a method that will make the Spatial Fleet independent of Earth's Ostler Beam. I don't know. I don't like it.

"Most likely we'll have war; and me, Jan-Shawan, with

three companions and seven offspring in Brez!"

He began a long harangue upon the many difficulties of a poor and down-trodden Port Officer. It was very evident that he was of the Martian Peace Party, wanted peace and plenty at any cost.

Grant winked at Gray.

"Of course, of course," he said soothingly, in an interval when Jan was recovering his spent breath. He leaned over and whispered something in the little man's ear, Gray saw the flicker of interchanging gold-edged credits.

The Martian hesitated, torn between cupidity and a strong sense of his own wounded honor, hesitated, and was lost. He wrote rapidly on a scrap of synthe-paper and handed it to Gray. "This will pass you through the guards, sir." He looked at the solemn Grant: "Remember, a personal favor only to you, Captain. For no other would I do this. I swear that." And to Gray: "Begone with you, my friend!"

Gray was gone.

Gray walked on impatient feet through the silent deserted streets of old Korna, ancient city of Mars. He passed jutting pillared buildings artificed in a weird un-Earthly style reaching up in silent majesty to the black sky. Side by side with these were evidences of an older, wiser civilization, garish night clubs, hybrids, maintained for the dubious benefit of unwary Terrestrial tourists, whose glaring midnight lights flung pools of white glow into the street.

But more often the twisting ways were dark and empty, illumined here and there by the dim red beam of a night lamp, or by the fitful glow of the racing Moons whirling by above. There were ominous rags of cloud in the dark sky, and the Moons played strange hide-and-seek among them. But the clouds were thickening, half covering the sky. There was a dull promise of coming storm in the electric air.

A promise of approaching storm that was both in the air here, Gray thought, and in the tightening relations of the worlds of Mars and Earth. If he but reached Gage's Palace in time, one storm might be averted. He quickened his already rapid pace.

At intervals he flung a searching glance along the length of narrow street behind him. Always he found emptiness, shadows, nothing that moved. But he was wary. Though it began increasingly to look as though the port blockade had baffled the efforts of the enemy, since so far he had proceeded unmolested, yet he did not allow the quiet to relax his vigilance. It might well be the ominous quiet before the storm. . . .

He swung round a darkened corner into the Street of the Palaces, took three steps in the direction of the ivory magnificence of the Terrestrial Mansion, and stopped dead, an involuntary cry of surprise wrung from his lips. For facing him was Edda, disheveled, panting, her dark eyes exotic pools of distress. She did not meet his glance.

"Edda! How did *you* get here?"

"I had to come. Jan-Shawan is an old friend of my father's, and I forced him to let me through. I had to come home tonight. My father—is very ill. And I thought I knew Korna, knew it as I know the streets of your own Washington. But I didn't. I lost myself, wandered in a panic, running. And I came here."

Gray's sudden suspicions had vanished, melted before her obvious distress. He said softly:

"Poor little thing! Lost! Well, you're not lost now. You'll come with me to your House of State, and we'll find where your father's house is. We—"

She was suddenly very white, face drained of all color.

"No, no! I couldn't go there! We'd lose too much time! I must go to my father—now! Oh, my dear, you will take me, won't you?"

She moved closer to him, soft mouth and lips subtly pleading. Gray looked at the scarlet bow of the parted lips and yielded inwardly. He took a half-step toward her, was reaching blindly to sweep her into the circle of his arms, when his glance moved up to her half-hidden eyes. And suddenly he recoiled, anger and horror mingled in his brain.

The eyes were savage, aflame, hot pools of all the blood-lust of the Scarlet Planet. The wild lure in them was the lure of exotic Mars, something subtly deadly and forbidden. Her lithe hand moved from under the protection of her cloak and lashed at him.

Horror choking him, he caught the slim ivory hand with the tiny knife glinting evilly in its stubborn grasp, tore the little weapon away, flung it in the street. She fought him like some captured wild animal.

"Edda!" he cried in horror, "Are you mad?"

She crumpled suddenly in his grasp, the murderous leaping flame gone from her dark eyes. Their jet pools were suddenly lacklustre and lifeless.

She said wearily, as he released her,

"I wish you would leave me now. I am tired. I have tried to do my father's bidding, obey his commands, and I have— failed. I am your K. I. agent. I am your attempted murderess. It was I who signaled that night from the *Trident's* helio-room, who made my excuses that I might be rid of you to do my work.... I hate you! I hate Earth! Go away, I tell you, and leave me. I do not want ever to see you again. Go away!"

Gray looked down at her, where she lay crumpled in a pitiful little heap on the street. He could not find it in his heart or brain to hate her. Yet the fascination she had held for him was gone, turned bitter cold. He could look at her without passion. And understand.

Mars was all to her that Earth meant to him. Home. Country. A proud heritage millenniums old. Something to die for, to hold sacred. Race!

But a curiosity was devouring him, and anger. This man, her father—after all, it was he who was at fault. She was not naturally the tigress. He remembered her words to Tauro: "I think—I think there must be something that we onlookers do not know, misunderstanding somewhere." Her father had aroused this madness in her. A great hatred for the man rose within him.

He leaned over Edda, shook her gently.

"Who is your father?"

She struck his hand away, spat at him.

"My father—my father was Boma.... You murderer!"

He was stunned by that. Boma! Boma, who was dead. Who had been destroyed utterly with the flaming wreck of his warship. He understood the girl's bitter hate. To her, he was the murderer of her father.

There could, then, be no possible reconciliation between them. This girl, a murderess! And he to her a murderer! It was a bitter jest of Fate, against two who might have.... No! He would leave her. She had friends certainly to whom she could go. All that pretense of not knowing Korna was utter sham, designed to draw him on to death.

He turned away, moved off slowly down the Street of Palaces, that ancient boulevard of Korna that runs into the Place of Kings. From here, Gage's Palace was not far. He went on, very slowly. And once, he turned and looked back. The crumpled shape of the girl was moving, standing erect. He saw her stare after him. And vanish into the street shadows. She was gone.

But he felt no exultation at his victory. Only a sudden feeling of utter weariness. He was very tired. But the pouch under his arm was safe now—which was all that really mattered, certainly.

He moved up the broad smooth steps of the Earth Palace. A spot of light from a photo-cell flickered on his face, ringing a soft bell somewhere back in the great house. He heard slow footsteps presently, and after a time a hastily attired manservant extended his ruffled head through the half-opened door. The man looked at Gray suspiciously.

"What do you want?"

"I've got to see the Ambassador," said Gray slowly. "Now. Take me to him at once. Or bring him down here. It makes no difference."

The servant was hesitating, uncertain. Gray pushed the man back and stepped into a darkened hall. The servant shut the door after him and retreated up the steps of a great stairway leading into the vague darkness of the second floor.

Presently Gray heard slow footsteps descending the stair and a petulant voice demanding:

"But what does the man want, Brentz?"

"I don't know, sir. But I will say he looks very suspicious to me, sir."

A switch clicked. Lights flashed on in the hall. And Gray faced a heavy grey-haired man of about sixty, dressed in a rumpled bath-robe and pajamas. Instinctively Gray knew that this was the Ambassador. A subtle aura of power clung about the man, was reflected in his gestures, in the keen glint of his sharp eyes.

Gray bowed, and handed Gage a certain letter signed by the Seal of the Earth State. The impatient frown on the heavy face changed into quick understanding. He looked at Gray a minute under heavy brows.

"You're the messenger, eh? The man from Earth that I expected?"

Gray nodded. "Yes."

"Come into the library, sir," said Gage; and to the servant: "You may go, Brentz." The man faded away discreetly.

In the library, a great high-ceilinged room with long dark rows of book shelves against the paneled walls, and with a brisk fire burning in the wide grate, Gray told his lengthy story. And when he had finished, he passed the pouch across to the eager hands of the Ambassador. He said dully:

"Do you think we have any sort of chance, sir?"

The Ambassador stared at him out of thoughtful eyes.

"We've got every chance, Gray. With Boma dead—" he did not notice the younger man wince— "with Boma dead and so of course unable to speak against us, I've no doubt that the Emperor's greed for water will overcome his desire for the radium. This message you've brought will win for us, Gray."

He stopped speaking suddenly, and stared. Gray had yielded to utter exhaustion at last, crumpled into the warm comfort of a soft chair. The Ambassador smiled, went over and picked him up in capable arms, carried him along the stairway into a great dark bedroom.

"You'll stay here tonight, Gray," the Ambassador said gravely. "Earth owes you more than she'll ever be able to repay."

Gray wanted to protest, but the strange sensation of sleeping in an Ambassador's bed had overcome his resistance. He was dead to the world.

The Ambassador went softly down into the lower hall again, and put in an emergency call for the Secretary of the Red Palace.

Some hours later, a space-liner bound from New Washington to the Polar Cities of Mars (via Korna), released from bondage by a terse edict from the Red Imperial Palace, lifted from her landing-cradle at the Space Port and rose slowly into the night sky. Her name glowed in luminous colors on her sleek dark hull. "S. L. TRIDENT—TERRESTRIAL."

And on her silent bridge, under the black-and-white pageant of the stars, her captain knocked out a last pipe and spoke reflectively to the night: "Gray must've gotten through.... Well, he always was a lucky devil!"